GADSBY

GADSBY

By

Ernest Vincent Wright

KNEES CALHOON

RAMBLE HOUSE

INTRODUCTION

THE ENTIRE MANUSCRIPT of this story was written with the E type-bar of the typewriter tied down; thus making it impossible for that letter to be printed. This was done so that none of that vowel might slip in, accidentally; and many did try to do so!

There is a great deal of information as to what Youth can do, if given a chance; and, though it starts out in somewhat of an impersonal vein, there is plenty of thrill, rollicking comedy, love, courtship, marriage, patriotism, sudden tragedy, a determined stand against liquor, and some amusing political aspirations in a small growing town.

In writing such a story—purposely avoiding all words containing the vowel E, there are a great many difficulties. The greatest of these is met in the past tense of verbs, almost all of which end with "—ed." Therefore substitutes must be found; and they are very few. This will cause, at times, a somewhat monotonous use of such words as "said;" for neither "replied," "answered" nor "asked" can be used. Another difficulty comes with the elimination of the common couplet "of course," and its very common connective, "consequently;" which will unavoidably cause "bumpy spots." The numerals also cause plenty of trouble, for none between six and thirty are available. When introducing young ladies into the story, this is a real barrier; for what young woman wants to have it known that she is over thirty? And this restriction on numbers, of course taboos all mention of dates.

Many abbreviations also must be avoided; the most common of all, "Mr." and "Mrs." being particularly troublesome; for those words, if read aloud, plainly indicate the E in their orthography.

As the vowel E is used more than five times oftener than any other letter, this story was written, not through any attempt to attain literary merit, but due to a somewhat balky nature, caused by hearing it so constantly claimed that "it can't be done; for you cannot say anything at all without using E, and make smooth continuity, with perfectly grammatical construction—" so 'twas said.

Many may think that I simply "drop" the E's, filling the gaps with apostrophes. A perusal of the book will show that this is not so. All words used are complete; are correctly spelled and properly used. This has been accomplished through the use of synonyms; and, by so twisting a sentence around as to avoid ambiguity. The book may prove a valuable aid to school children in English composition.

People, as a rule, will not stop to realize what a task such an attempt actually is. As I wrote along, in long-hand at first, a whole army of little E's gathered around my desk, all eagerly expecting to be called upon. But gradually as they saw me writing on and on, without even noticing them, they grew uneasy; and, with excited whisperings amongst themselves, began hopping up and riding on my pen, looking down constantly for a chance to drop off into some word; for all the world like sea-birds perched, watching for a passing fish! But when they saw that I had covered 138 pages of typewriter size paper, they slid off onto the floor, walking sadly away, arm in arm; but shouting back:

"You certainly must have a hodge-podge of a yarn there without Us! Why, man! We are in every story ever written, hundreds of thousands of times! This is the first time we ever were shut out!"

Pronouns also caused trouble; for such words as he, she, they, them, theirs, her, herself, myself, himself, yourself, etc., could not be utilized. But a particularly annoying obstacle comes when, almost through a long paragraph you can find no words with which to continue that line of thought; hence, as in Solitaire, you are "stuck," and must go way back and start another; which, of course, must perfectly fit the preceding context.

I have received some extremely odd criticisms since the Associated Press widely announced that such a book was being written. A rapid-talking New York newspaper columnist wanted to know how I would get over the plain fact that my name contains the letter E three times. As an author's name is not a part of his story, that criticism did not hold water. And I received one most scathing epistle from a lady (woman!) denouncing me as a "genuine fake;" (that paradox being a most interesting one!), and ending by saying:—"Everyone knows that such a feat is impossible." All right. Then the impossible has been accomplished; (a paradox to equal hers!) Other criticism may be directed at the Introduction; but this section of a story also is not part of it. The author is entitled to it, in order properly to explain his work. The story required five and a half months of concentrated endeavor, with so many erasures and retrenchments that I tremble as I think of them. Of course anybody can write such a story. All that is needed is a piece of string tied from the E type-bar down to some part of the base of the typewriter. Then simply go ahead and type your story. Incidentally, you should have some sort of a bromide preparation handy, for use when the going gets rough, as it most assuredly will!

Before the book was in print, I was freely and openly informed "there is a trick, or catch, somewhere in that claim that there is not one letter E in the entire book, after you leave the Introduction. Well; it is the privilege of the reader to unearth any such deception that he or she may think they can find. I have even ordered the printer not to head each chapter with the words "Chapter 2," etc., on account of that bothersome E in that word.

In closing let me say that I trust you may learn to love all the young folks in the story, as deeply as I have, in introducing them to you. Like many a book, it grows more and more interesting as the reader becomes well acquainted with the characters.

Ernest Vincent Wright
Los Angeles, California
February, 1939

GADSBY

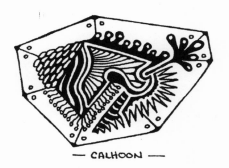

— CALHOON —

IF YOUTH, THROUGHOUT all history, had had a champion to stand up for it; to show a doubting world that a child can think; and, possibly, do it practically; you wouldn't constantly run across folks today who claim that "a child don't know anything." A child's brain starts functioning at birth; and has, amongst its many infant convolutions, thousands of dormant atoms, into which God has put a mystic possibility for noticing an adult's act, and figuring out its purport.

Up to about its primary school days a child thinks, naturally, only of play. But many a form of play contains disciplinary factors. "You can't do this," or "that puts you out," shows a child that it must think, practically or fail. Now, if, throughout childhood, a brain has no opposition, it is plain that it will attain a position of "status quo," as with our ordinary animals. Man knows not why a cow, dog or lion was not born with a brain on a par with ours; why such animals cannot add, subtract, or obtain from books and schooling, that paramount position which Man holds today.

But a human brain is not in that class. Constantly throbbing and pulsating, it rapidly forms opinions; attaining an ability of its own; a fact which is startlingly shown by an occasional child "prodigy" in music or school work. And as, with our dumb animals, a child's inability convincingly to impart its thoughts to us, should not class it as ignorant.

Upon this basis I am going to show you how a bunch of bright young folks did find a champion; a man with boys and girls of his own; a man of so dominating and happy individuality that Youth is drawn to him as is a fly to a sugar bowl. It is a story about a small town. It is not a gossipy yarn; nor is it a dry, monotonous account, full of such customary "fill-ins" as "romantic moonlight casting murky shadows down a long, winding country road." Nor will it say anything about tinklings lulling distant folds; robins caroling at twilight, nor any "warm glow of lamplight" from a cabin window. No. It is an account of up-and-doing activity; a vivid portrayal of Youth as it is today; and a practical discarding of that worn-out notion that "a child don't know anything."

Now, any author, from history's dawn, always had that most important aid to writing: an ability to call upon any word in his dictionary in building up his story. That is, our strict laws as to word construction did not block his path. But in my story that mighty obstruction will constantly stand in my path; for many an important, common word I cannot adopt, owing to its orthography.

I shall act as a sort of historian for this small town; associating with its inhabitants, and striving to acquaint you with its youths, in such a way that you can look, knowingly, upon any child, rich or poor; forward or "backward"; your own, or John Smith's, in your community. You will find many young minds aspiring to know how, and WHY such a thing is so. And, if a child shows curiosity in that way, how ridiculous it is for you to snap out:—"Oh! Don't ask about things too old for you!"

Such a jolt to a young child's mind, craving instruction, is apt so to dull its avidity, as to hold it back in its school work. Try to look upon a child as a small, soft young body and a rapidly growing, constantly inquiring brain. It must grow to maturity slowly. Forcing a child through school by constant night study during hours in which it should run and play, can bring on insomnia; handicapping both brain and body.

Now this small town in our story had grown in just that way:— slowly; in fact, much too slowly to stand on a par with many a thousand of its kind in this big, vigorous nation of ours. It was simply stagnating; just as a small mountain brook, coming to a hollow, might stop, and sink from sight, through not having a will to find a way through that obstruction; or around it. You will run across such a dormant town, occasionally; possibly so dormant that only outright isolation by a fast-moving world, will show it its folly. If you will tour Asia, Yucatan, or parts of Africa and Italy, you will find many sad ruins of past kingdoms. Go to Indo-China and visit its gigantic Ankhor Wat; call at Damascus, Baghdad and Samarkand. What sorrowful lack of ambition many such a community shows in thus discarding such high-class construction! And I say, again, that so will Youth grow dormant, and hold this big, throbbing world back, if no champion backs it up; thus providing it with an opportunity to show its ability for looking forward, and improving unsatisfactory conditions.

So this small town of Branton Hills was lazily snoozing amidst up-and-doing towns, as Youth's Champion, John Gadsby, took hold of it; and shook its dawdling, flabby body until its inhabitants thought a tornado had struck it. Call it tornado, volcano, military onslaught, or what you will, this town found that it had a bunch of kids who had wills that would admit of no snoozing; for that is Youth, on its forward march of inquiry, thought and action.

If you stop to think of it, you will find that it is customary for our "grown-up" brain to cast off many of its functions of its youth; and to think only of what it calls "topics of maturity." Amongst such discards is many a form of happy play; many a muscular activity such as walking, running, climbing; thus totally missing that alluring "joy of living" of childhood. If you wish a vacation from financial affairs, just go out and play with Youth. Play "blind-man's buff," "hop-scotch," "ring toss," and football. Go out to a charming woodland spot on a picnic with a bright, happy, vivacious group. Sit down at a corn roast; a marshmallow toast; join in singing popular songs; drink a quart of good, rich milk; burrow into that big lunch box; and all such things as banks, stocks, and family bills, will vanish on fairy wings, into oblivion.

But this is not a claim that Man should stay always youthful. Supposing that that famous Spaniard, landing upon Florida's coral strands, had found that mythical Fountain of Youth; what a calamity for mankind! A world without maturity of thought; without man's full-grown muscular ability to construct mighty buildings, railroads and ships; a world without authors, doctors, savants, musicians; nothing but Youth! I can think of but a solitary approval of such a condition; for such a horror as war would not, could not occur; for a child is, naturally, a small bunch of sympathy. I know that boys will "scrap;" also that "spats" will occur amongst girls; but, at such a monstrosity as killings by bombing towns, sinking ships, or mass annihilation of marching troops, childhood would stand aghast. Not a tiny bird would fall; nor would any form of gun nor facility for manufacturing it, insult that almost Holy purity of youthful thought. Anybody who knows that wracking sorrow brought upon a child by a dying puppy or cat, knows that childhood can show us that our fighting, our policy of "a tooth for a tooth," is abominably wrong.

So, now to start our story.

Branton Hills was a small town in a rich agricultural district; and having many a possibility for growth. But, through a sort of smug satisfaction with conditions of long ago, had no thought of improving such important adjuncts as roads; putting up public buildings, nor laying out parks; in fact a dormant, slowly dying community. So satisfactory was its status that it had no form of transportation to surrounding towns but by railroad, or "old Dobbin." Now, any town thus isolating its inhabitants, will invariably find this big, busy world passing it by; glancing at it, curiously, as at an odd animal at a circus; and, you will find, caring not a whit about its condition. Naturally, a town should grow. You can look upon it as a child; which, through natural conditions, should attain manhood; and add to its surrounding thriving districts its products of farm, shop, or factory. It should show a spirit of association with surrounding towns; crawl out of its lair, and find how backward it is.

Now, in all such towns, you will find, occasionally, an individual born with that sort of brain which, knowing that his town is backward, longs to start things toward improving it; not only its living conditions, but adding an institution or two, such as any city, big or small, maintains, gratis, for its inhabitants. But so forward looking a man finds that trying to instill any such notions into a town's ruling body is about as satisfactory as butting against a brick wall. Such "Boards" as you find ruling many a small town, function from such a soporific rut that any hint of digging cash from its cast iron strong box with its big brass padlock, will fall upon minds as rigid as rock.

Branton Hills had such a man, to whom such rigidity was as annoying as a thorn in his foot. Continuous trials brought only continual thornpricks; until, finally, a brilliant plan took form as John Gadsby found Branton Hills' High School pupils waking up to Branton Hills' sloth. Gadsby continually found this bright young bunch asking:— "Aw! Why is this town so slow? It's nothing but a dry twig!!"

"Ha!" said Gadsby; "A dry twig! That's it! Many a living, blossoming branch all around us, and this solitary dry twig, with a tag hanging from it, on which you will find: 'Branton Hills; A twig too lazy to grow!' "

Now this put a "hunch" in Gadsby's brain, causing him to say: "A High School pupil is not a child, now. Naturally a High School boy has not a man's qualifications; nor has a High School girl womanly maturity. But such kids, born in this swiftly moving day, think out many a notion which will work, but which would pass our dads and granddads in cold disdain. Just as ships pass at night. But supposing that such ships should show a light in passing; or blow a horn; or, if—if—if—By Golly! I'll do it!"

And so Gadsby sat on his blossom-bound porch on a mild Spring morning, thinking and smoking. Smoking can calm a man down; and his thoughts had so long and so constantly clung to this plan of his that a cool outlook as to its promulgation was not only important, but paramount. So, as his cigar was whirling and puffing rings aloft; and as groups of bright, happy boys and girls trod past, to school, his plan rapidly took form as follows:—"Youth! What is it? Simply a start. A start of what? Why, of that most astounding of all human functions; thought. But man didn't start his brain working. No. All that an adult can claim is a continuation, or an amplification of thoughts, dormant in his youth. Although a child's brain can absorb instruction with an ability far surpassing that of a grown man; and, although such a young brain is bound by rigid limits, it contains a capacity for constantly craving additional facts. So, in our backward Branton Hills, I just know that I can find boys and girls who can show our old moss-back Town Hall big-wigs a thing or two. Why! On Town Hall night, just go and sit in that room and find out just how stupid and stubborn a Council, (put into Town Hall, you know, through popular ballot!), can act. Say that a road is badly worn. Shall it stay so? Up jumps Old Bill Simpkins claiming that it is a townsman's duty to fix up his wagon springs if that road is too rough for him!"

As Gadsby sat thinking thus, his plan was rapidly growing: and, in a month, was actually starting to work. How? You'll know shortly; but first, you should know this John Gadsby; a man of "around fifty;" a family man, and known throughout Branton Hills for his high standard of honor and altruism on any kind of an occasion for public good. A loyal churchman, Gadsby was a man who, though admitting that an occasional fault in our daily acts is bound to occur, had taught his two boys and a pair of girls that, though folks do slip from what Scriptural authors call that "straight and narrow path," it will not pay to risk your own Soul by slipping, just so that you can laugh at your ability in staying out of prison; for Gadsby, having grown up in Branton Hills, could point to many such man or woman. So, with such firm convictions in his mind, this upstanding man was constantly striving so to act that no complaint from man, woman or child should bring a word of disapproval. In his mind, what a man might do was that man's affair only and could stain no Soul but his own. And his altruism taught that it is not difficult to find many ways in which to bring joy to such as cannot, through physical disability, go out to look for it; and that only a small bit of joy, brought to a shut-in invalid will carry with it such a warmth as can flow only from acts of human sympathy.

For many days Gadsby had thought of ways in which folks with a goodly bank account could aid in building up this rapidly backsliding town of contribution could do? In this town, full of capitalists and philanthropists contributing, off and on, for shipping warming pans to Zulus, Gadsby saw a solution. In whom? Why, in just that bunch of bright, happy school kids, back from many a visit to a city, and noting its ability in improving its living conditions. So Gadsby thought of thus carrying an inkling to such capitalists as to how this stagnating town could claim a big spot upon our national map, which is now shown only in small, insignificant print.

As a start, Branton Hills' "Daily Post" would carry a long story, outlining a list of factors for improving conditions. This it did; but it will always stay as a blot upon high minds and proud blood that not a man or woman amongst such capitalists saw, in his plan, any call for dormant funds. But did that stop Gadsby? Can you stop a rising wind? Hardly So Gadsby took into council about forty boys of his vicinity and built up an Organization of Youth. Also about as many girls who had known what it is, compulsorily to pass up many a picnic, or various forms of sport, through a lack of public park land. So this strong, vigorous combination of both youth and untiring activity, avidly took up Gadsby's plan; for nothing so stirs up a youthful mind as an opportunity for accomplishing anything that adults cannot do. And did Gadsby know Youth? I'll say so! His two sons and girls, now in High or Grammar school, had taught him a thing or two; principal amongst which was that all-dominating fact that, at a not too far distant day, our young folks will occupy important vocational and also political positions, and will look back upon this, our day; smiling kindly at our way of doing things. So, to say that many a Branton Hills "King of Capital" got a bit huffy as a High School stripling was proving how stubborn a rich man is if his dollars don't aid so vast an opportunity for doing good, would put it mildly! Such downright gall by a half-grown kid to inform him; an outstanding light on Branton Hills' tax list, that this town was sliding down hill; and would soon land in an abyss of national oblivion! And our Organization girls! How Branton Hills' rich old widows and plump matrons did sniff in disdain as a group of High School pupils brought forth straightforward claims that cash paving a road, is doing good practical work, but, in filling up a strong box, is worth nothing to our town.

Oh, that class of nabobs! How thoroughly Gadsby did know its parsimony!! And how thoroughly did this hard-planning man know just what a constant onslaught by Youth could do. So, in about a month, his "Organization" had "waylaid," so to say, practically half of Branton Hills' cash kings; and had so won out, through that commonly known "pull" upon an adult by a child asking for what plainly is worthy, that his mail brought not only cash, but two rich landlords put at his disposal, tracts of land "for any form of occupancy which can, in any way, aid our town." This land Gadsby's Organization promptly put into growing farm products for gratis distribution to Branton Hills' poor; and that burning craving of Youth for activity soon had it sprouting corn, squash, potato, onion and asparagus crops; and, to "doll it up a bit," put in a patch of blossoming plants.

Naturally any man is happy at a satisfactory culmination of his plans and so, as Gadsby found that public philanthropy was but an affair of plain, ordinary approach, it did not call for much brain work to find that, possibly also, a way might turn up for putting handicraft instruction in Branton Hills' schools; for schooling, according to him, did not consist only of books and black-boards. Hands, also should know how to construct various practical things in woodwork, plumbing, blacksmithing, masonry, and so forth; with thorough instruction in sanitation, and that most important of all youthful activity, gymnastics. For girls such a school could instruct in cooking, suit making, hat making, fancy work, art and loom-work; in fact, about any handicraft that a girl might wish to study, and which is not in our standard school curriculum. But as Gadsby thought of such a school, no way for backing it financially was in sight. Town funds naturally, should carry it along; but town funds and Town Councils do not always form what you might call—synonymous words. So it was compulsory that cash should actually "drop into his lap," via a continuation of solicitations by his now grandly functioning Organization of Youth. So, out again trod that bunch of bright, happy kids, putting forth such plain, straightforward facts as to what Manual Training would do for Branton Hills, that many saw it in that light. But you will always find a group, or individual complaining that such things would "automatically dawn" on boys and girls without any training. Old Bill Simpkins was loud in his antagonism to what was a "crazy plan to dip into our town funds just to allow boys to saw up good wood, and girls to burn up good flour, trying to cook biscuits." Kids, according to him, should go to work in Branton Hills' shopping district, and profit by it.

"Bah! Why not start a class to show goldfish how to waltz! I didn't go to any such school; and what am I now? A Councilman! I can't saw a board straight, nor fry a potato chip; but I can show you folks how to hang onto your town funds."

Old Bill was a notorious grouch; but our Organization occasionally did find a totally varying mood. Old Lady Flanagan, with four boys in school, and a husband many days too drunk to work, was loud in approval.

"Whoops! Thot's phwat I calls a grand thing! Worra, worra! I wish Old Man Flanagan had had sich an opporchunity. But thot ignorant old clod don't know nuthin' but boozin', tobacca shmokin' and ditch-diggin'. And you know thot our Council ain't a-payin' for no ditch-scoopin' right now. So I'll shout for thot school! For my boys can find out how to fix thot barn door our old cow laid down against."

Ha, ha! What a circus our Organization had with such varying moods and outlooks! But, finally such a school was built; instructors brought in from surrounding towns; and Gadsby was as happy as a cat with a ball of yarn.

As Branton Hills found out what it can accomplish if it starts out with vigor and a will to win, our Organization thought of laying out a big park; furnishing an opportunity for small tots to romp and play on grassy plots; a park for all sorts of sports, picnics, and so forth; sand pots for babyhood; cozy arbors for girls who might wish to study, or talk. (You might, possibly, find a girl who can talk, you know!); also shady nooks and winding paths for old folks who might find comfort in such. Gadsby thought that a park is truly a most important adjunct to any community; for, if a growing population has no out-door spot at which its glooms, slumps and morbid thoughts can vanish upon wings of sunlight, amidst bright colorings of shrubs and sky, it may sink into a grouchy, faultfinding, squabbling group; and making such a showing for surrounding towns as to hold back any gain in population or valuation. Gadsby had a goodly plot of land in a grand location for a park and sold it to Branton Hills for a dollar; that stingy Council to lay it out according to his plans. And how his Organization did applaud him for this, his first "solo work!"

But schools and parks do not fulfill all of a town's calls. Many minds of varying kinds will long for an opportunity for finding out things not ordinarily taught in school. So Branton Hills' Public Library was found too small. As it was now in a small back room in our High School, it should occupy its own building; down town, and handy for all; and with additional thousands of books and maps. Now, if you think Gadsby and his youthful assistants stood aghast at such a gigantic proposition, you just don't know Youth, as it is today. But to whom could Youth look for so big an outlay as a library building would cost? Books also cost; librarians and janitors draw pay. So, with light, warmth, and all-round comforts, it was a task to stump a full-grown politician; to say nothing of a plain, ordinary townsman and a bunch of kids. So Gadsby thought of taking two bright boys and two smart girls to Washington, to call upon a man in a high position, who had got it through Branton Hills' popular ballot. Now, any politician is a convincing orator. (That is, you know, all that politics consists of!) and this big man, in contact with a visiting capitalist, looking for a handout for his own district, got a donation of a thousand dollars. But that wouldn't start a public library; to say nothing of maintaining it. So, back in Branton Hills, again, our Organization was out, as usual, on its war-path.

Branton Hills' philanthropy was now showing signs of monotony; so our Organization had to work its linguistic ability and captivating tricks full blast, until that thousand dollars had so grown that a library was built upon a vacant lot which had grown nothing but grass; and only a poor quality of it, at that; and many a child and adult quickly found ways of profitably passing odd hours.

Naturally Old Bill Simpkins was snooping around, sniffing and snorting at any signs of making Branton Hills "look cityish," (a word originating in Bill's vocabulary.)

"Huh!! I didn't put in any foolish hours with books in my happy childhood in this good old town! But I got along all right; and am now having my say in its Town Hall doings. Books!! Pooh! Maps! BAH!! It's silly to squat in a hot room squinting at a lot of print! If you want to know about a thing, go to work in a shop or factory of that kind, and find out about it first-hand."

"But, Bill," said Gadsby, "shops want a man who knows what to do without having to stop to train him."

"Oh, that's all bosh! If a boss shows a man what a tool is for; and if that man is any good, at all, why bring up this stuff you call training? That man grabs a tool, works 'til noon; knocks off for an hour; works 'til—"

At this point in Bill's blow-up an Italian Councilman was passing, and put in his oar, with:—

"Ha, Bill! You thinka your man can worka all right, firsta day, huh? You talka crazy so much for my boota! You lasta just a half hour. Thisa library all righta. This town too mucha what I call tight-wad!"

Oh, hum!! It's a tough job making old dogs do tricks. But our Organization was now holding almost daily sittings, and soon a bright girl thought of having band music in that now popular park. And what do you think that stingy Council did? It actually built a most fantastic band-stand; got a contract with a first-class band, and all without so much as a Councilman fainting away!! So, finally, on a hot July Sunday, two solid hours of grand harmony brought joy to many a poor Soul who had not for many a day, known that balm of comfort which can "air out our brains' dusty corridors," and bring such happy thrills, as Music, that charming Fairy, which knows no human words, can bring. Around that gaudy band-stand, at two-thirty on that first Sunday, sat or stood as happy a throng of old and young as any man could wish for; and Gadsby and his "gang" got hand-clasps and hand-claps, from all. A good band, you know, not only can stir and thrill you; for it can play a soft crooning lullaby, a lilting waltz or polka; or, with its wood winds, bring forth old songs of our childhood, ballads of courting days, or hymns and carols of Christmas; and can suit all sorts of folks, in all sorts of moods; for a Spaniard, Dutchman or Russian can find similar joy with a man from Italy, Norway or far away Brazil.

BY NOW, BRANTON HILLS was so proud of not only its "smarting up," but also of its startling growth, on that account, that an application was put forth for its incorporation as a city; a small city, naturally, but full of that condition of Youth, known as "growing pains." So its shabby old "Town Hall" sign was thrown away, and a black and gold onyx slab, with "CITY HALL" blazing forth in vivid colors, put up, amidst band music, flag waving, parading and oratory. In only a month from that glorious day, Gadsby found folks ''primping up''; girls putting on bright ribbons boys finding that suits could stand a good ironing; and rich widows and portly matrons almost outdoing any rainbow in brilliancy. An occasional shop along Broadway, which had a rattly door or shaky windows was put into first class condition, to fit Branton Hills' status as a city. Old Bill Simpkins was strutting around, as pompous as a drum-major; for, now, that old Town Council would function as a CITY council; HIS council! His own stamping ground! According to him, from it, at no far day, "Bill Simpkins, City Councilman," would show an anxiously waiting world how to run a city; though probably, I think, how *not* to run it.

It is truly surprising what a narrow mind, what a blind outlook a man, brought up with practically no opposition to his boyhood wants, can attain; though brought into contact with indisputably important data for improving his city. Our Organization boys thought Bill *"a bit off"* but Gadsby would only laugh at his blasts against paying out city funds; for, you know, all bombs don't burst; you occasionally find a "dud."

But this furor for fixing up rattly doors or shaky windows didn't last; for Old Bill's oratory found favor with a bunch of his old tight-wads, who actually thought of inaugurating a campaign against Gadsby's Organization of Youth. As soon as this was known about town, that mythical pot, known as Public Opinion, was boiling furiously. A vast majority stood back of Gadsby and his kids; so, old Bill's ranks could count only on a small group of rich old Shylocks to whom a bank-book was a thing to look into or talk about only annually; that is, on bank-balancing days. This small minority got up a slogan:— "Why Spoil a Good Old Town?" and actually did, off and on, talk a shopman out of fixing up his shop or grounds. This, you know, put additional vigor into our Organization; inspiring a boy to bring up a plan for calling a month—say July—"pick-up, paint-up and wash-up month;" for it was a plain fact that, all about town, was many a shabby spot; a lot of buildings could stand a good coat of paint, and yards raking up; thus showing surrounding towns that not only *could* Branton Hills "doll up," but had a class of inhabitants who gladly would go at such a plan, and carry it through. So Gadsby got his "gang" out, to sally forth and any man or woman who did not jump, at first, at such a plan by vigorous Youth, was always brought around, through noticing how poorly a shabby yard did look. So Gadsby put in Branton Hills' "Post" this stirring call:—

"Raking up your yard or painting your building is simply improving it both in worth; artistically and from a utilization standpoint. I know that many a city front lawn is small; but, if it is only fairly big, a walk, cut curvingly, will add to it, surprisingly. That part of a walk which runs to your front door could show rows of small rocks rough and natural; and grading from small to big; but *no* 'hit-or-miss' layout. You can so fix up your yard as to form an approach to unity in plan with such as adjoin you; though without actual duplication; thus providing harmony for all who may pass by.

It is, in fact, but a bit of City Planning; and anybody who aids in such work is a most worthy inhabitant. So, *cut* your scraggly lawns! *Trim* your old, shaggy shrubs! Bring into artistic form, your grass-grown walks!"

(Now, naturally, in writing such a story as this, with its conditions as laid down in its Introduction, it is not surprising that an occasional "rough spot" in composition is found. So I trust that a critical public will hold constantly in mind that I am voluntarily avoiding words containing that symbol which is, *by far,* of most common inclusion in writing our Anglo-Saxon as it is, today. Many of our most common words cannot show; so I must adopt synonyms; and so twist a thought around as to say what I wish with as much clarity as I can.)

So, now to go on with this odd contraption:

By Autumn, a man who took his vacation in July, would hardly know his town upon coming back, so thoroughly had thousands "dug in" to aid in its transformation.

"Boys," said Gadsby. "you can pat your own backs, if you can't find anybody to do it for you. This city is proud of you. And, girls, just sing with joy; for not only is your city proud of you, but I am, too."

"But how about you, sir, and your work?"

This was from Frank; a boy brought up to think fairly on all things. "Oh," said Gadsby laughingly, "I didn't do much of anything but boss you young folks around. If our Council awards any diplomas, I don't want any. I would look ridiculous strutting around with a diploma with a pink ribbon on it, now wouldn't I!"

This talk of diplomas was as a bolt from a bright sky to this young, hustling bunch. But, though Gadsby's words did sound as though a grown man wouldn't want such a thing, that wasn't saying that a young boy or girl wouldn't; and with this surprising possibility ranking in young minds, many a kid was in an anti-soporific condition for parts of many a night.

But a kindly Councilman actually did bring up a bill about this diploma affair, and his collaborators put it through; which naturally brought up talk as how to award such diplomas. At last it was thought that a big public affair at City Hall, with our Organization on a platform, with Branton Hills' Mayor and Council, would furnish an all-round, satisfactory way.

Such an occasion was worthy of a lot of planning; and a first thought was for flags and bunting on all public buildings; with a grand illumination at night. Stationary lights should glow from all points on which a light could stand, hang, or swing; and gigantic rays should swoop and swish across clouds and sky. Bands should play; boys and girls march and sing; and a vast crowd would pour into City Hall. As on similar occasions, a bad rush for chairs was apt to occur, a company of military units should occupy all important points, to hold back anything simulating a jam.

Now, if you think our Organization wasn't all agog and wild, with youthful anticipation at having a diploma for work out of school hours, you just don't know Youth. Boys and girls, though not full grown inhabitants of a city, do know what will add to its popularity; and having had a part in bringing about such conditions, it was but natural to look back upon such, as any military man might at winning a difficult fight.

So, finally our big day was at hand! That it might not cut into school hours, it was on a Saturday; and, by noon, about a thousand kids, singing, shouting and waving flags, stood in formation at City Park, awaiting with growing thrills, a signal which would start as big a turn-out as Branton Hills had known in all its history. Up at City Hall awaiting arrivals of city officials, a big crowd sat; row upon row of chairs which not only took up all floor room, but also many a small spot, in doorway or on a balcony in which a chair or stool could find footing; and all who could not find such an opportunity willingly stood in back. Just as a group of officials sat down on that flag-bound platform, distant throbbing of drums, and bright, snappy band music told of Branton Hills approaching thousands of kids, who, finally marching in through City Hall's main door, stood in a solid mass around that big room.

Naturally Gadsby had to put his satisfaction into words; and, advancing to a mahogany stand, stood waiting for a storm of hand-clapping and shouts to quit, and said:—

"Your Honor, Mayor of Branton Hills, its Council, and all you out in front:—If you would only stop rating a child's ability by your own; and try to find out just *what* ability a child has, our young folks throughout this big world would show a surprisingly willing disposition to try things which would bring your approbation. A child's brain is an astonishing thing. It has, in its construction, an astounding capacity for absorbing what is brought to it; and not only to think about, but to find ways for improving it. It is today's child who, tomorrow, will, you know, laugh at our ways of doing things. So, in putting across this campaign of building up our community into a municipality which has won acclaim, not only from its officials and inhabitants, but from surrounding towns I found, in our young folks, an out-and-out inclination to assist; and you, today, can look upon it as labor in which your adult aid was but a small factor. So now, my Organization of Youth, if you will pass across this platform, your Mayor will hand you your diplomas."

Not in all Branton Hills' history had any boy or girl known such a thrill as upon winning that hard-won roll! And from solid banks of humanity roars of congratulation burst forth. As soon as Mayor Brown shook hands (and such tiny, warm, soft young hands, too!) with all, a big out-door lunch was found waiting on a charming lawn back of City Hall; and this was no World War mobilization lunch of doughnuts and a hot dog sandwich; but, as two of Gadsby's sons said, was an all-round, good, big fill-up;" and many a boy's and girl's "tummy" was soon as round and taut as a balloon.

As twilight was turning to dusk, boys in an adjoining lot shot skyward a crashing bomb, announcing a grand illumination as a fitting climax for so glorious a day; and thousands sat on rock-walls, grassy knolls, in cars or at windows, with a big crowd standing along curbs and crosswalks. Myriads of lights of all colors, in solid balls, sprays, sparkling fountains, and bursts of glory, shot, in criss-cross paths, up and down, back and forth, across a star-lit sky; providing a display without a par in local annals.

But not only did Youth thrill at so fantastic a show. Adults had many a Fourth of July brought back from a distant past; in which our national custom wound up our most important holiday with a similar display; only, in our Fourths of long ago, horrifying, gigantic concussions would disturb old folks and invalids until midnight; at which hour, according to *law,* all such carrying-on must stop. But did it? Possibly in *your* town, but not around my district! All Fourth of July outfits don't always function at first, you know; and no kid, (or adult!) would think of quitting until that last pop should pop; or that last bang should bang. And so, many a dawn on July fifth found things still going, full blast.

YOUTH CANNOT STAY for long in a condition of inactivity; and so, for only about a month did things so stand, until a particularly bright girl in our Organization, thought out a plan for caring for infants of folks who had to go out, to work; and this bright kid soon had a group of girls who would join, during vacation, in voluntarily giving up four days a month to such work. With about fifty girls collaborating, all districts had this most gracious aid; and a girl would not only watch and guard, but would also instruct, as far as practical, any such tot as had not had its first schooling. Such work by young girls still in school was a grand thing; and Gadsby not only stood up for such loyalty, but got at his boys to find a similar plan; and soon had a full troop of Boy Scouts; uniforms and all. This automatically brought about a Girl Scout unit; and, through a collaboration of both, a form of club sprang up. It was a club in which any boy or girl of a family owning a car would call mornings for pupils having no cars, during school days, for a trip to school and back. This was not only a saving in long walks for many, but also took from a young back, that hard, tiring strain from lugging such armfuls of books as you find pupils laboriously carrying, today. Upon arriving at a school building, many cars would unload so many books that Gadsby said:——

"You would think that a Public Library branch was moving in!" This car work soon brought up a thought of giving similar aid to ailing adults; who, not owning a car, could not know of that vast display of hill and plain so common to a majority of our townsfolks. So a plan was laid, by which a car would call two days a month; and for an hour or so, follow roads winding out of town and through woods, farm lands and suburbs; showing distant ponds, and that grand arch of sky which "shut-ins" know only from photographs. Ah; *how* that plan did stir up joyous anticipation amongst such as thus had an opportunity to call upon old, loving pals, and talk of old customs and past days! Occasionally such a talk would last so long that a youthful motorist, waiting dutifully at a curb, thought that a full family history of both host and visitor was up for an airing. But old folks always *will* talk and it will not do a boy or girl any harm to wait; for, you know, that boy or girl will act in just that way, at a not too far-off day!

But, popular as this touring plan was, it had to stop; for school again took all young folks from such out-door activity. Nobody was so sorry at this as Gadsby, for though Branton Hills' suburban country is glorious from March to August, it is also strong in its attractions throughout Autumn, with its artistic colorings of fruits, pumpkins, corn-shocks, hay-stacks and Fall blossoms. So Gadsby got a big motor-coach company to run a bus a day, carrying, gratis, all poor or sickly folks who had a doctor's affidavit that such an outing would aid in curing ills arising from too constant in-door living; and so, up almost to Thanksgiving, this big coach ran daily.

As Spring got around again, this "man-of-all-work" thought of driv-
ing away a shut-in invalid's monotony by having musicians go to such
rooms, to play; or, by taking along a vocalist or trio, sing such old
songs as always bring back happy days. This work Gadsby thought of
paying for by putting on a circus. And *was* it a circus? *It was!!* It had
boys forming both front and hind limbs of animals totally unknown to
zoology; girls strutting around as gigantic birds of also doubtful origin;
an array of small living animals such as trick dogs and goats, a dancing
pony, a group of imitation Indians, cowboys, cowgirls, a kicking trick
jack-ass; and, talk about clowns! Forty boys got into baggy pantaloons
and fools' caps; and no circus, including that first of all shows in
Noah's Ark, had so much going on. Gymnasts from our school gymna-
sium, tumbling, jumping and racing; comic dancing; a clown band;
high-swinging artists, and a funny cop who didn't wait to find out who
a man was, but hit him anyway. And, as no circus *is* a circus without
boys shouting wildly about pop-corn and cold drinks, Gadsby saw to it
that such boys got in as many patrons way as any ambitious youth
could; and that is "going strong," if you know boys, at all!

But what about profits? It not only paid for all acts which his Organization couldn't put on, but it was found that a big fund for many a
day's musical visitations, was on hand.

And, now a word or two about municipal affairs in this city; or any
city, in which nobody will think of doing anything about its poor and
sick, without a vigorous prodding up. City Councils, now-a-days, willingly grant big appropriations for paving, lights, schools, jails, courts,
and so on; but invariably fight shy of charity; which is nothing but
sympathy for anybody who is "down and out."

No man can say that Charity will not, during coming days, aid *him* in
supporting his family; and it was Gadsby's claim that *humans:—not
blocks of buildings,* form what Mankind calls a city. But what would
big, costly buildings amount to, if all who work in such cannot maintain that good physical condition paramount in carrying on a city's
various forms of labor? And not only *physical* good, but also a mind
happy from lack of worry and of that stagnation which always follows
a monotonous daily grind. So our Organization was soon out again,
agitating City Officials and civilians toward building a big Auditorium
in which all kinds of shows and sports could occur, with also a swim-
ming pool and hot and cold baths. Such a building cannot so much as
start without financial backing; but gradually many an iron-bound bank

account was drawn upon (much as you pull a tooth!), to buy bonds. Also, such a building won't grow up in a night; nor was a spot upon which to put it found without a lot of agitation; many wanting it in a down-town district; and also, many who had vacant land put forth all sorts of claims to obtain cash for lots upon which a big tax was paid annually, with-out profits. But all such things automatically turn out satisfactorily to a majority; though an ugly, squawk that "municipal graft" was against him.

Now Gadsby was vigorously against graft; not only in city affairs but in any kind of transaction; and that stab brought forth such a flow of oratory from him, that as voting for Mayor was soon to occur, it, and a long list of good works, soon had him up for that position. But Gadsby didn't want such a nomination; still, thousands of towns-folks who had known him from childhood, would not hark to anything but his candidacy; and, soon, on window cards, signs, and flags across Broadway, was his photograph and **"GADSBY FOR MAYOR"**; and a campaign was on which still rings in Branton Hills' history as "hot stuff!" Four aspiring politicians ran in opposition; and, as all had good backing, and Gadsby only his public works to fall back on, things soon got looking gloomy for him. His antagonists, standing upon soap box, auto truck, or hastily built platforms, put forth, with prodigious vim, claims that "our fair city will go back to its original oblivion if *I* am not its Mayor!" But our Organization now took a hand, most of which, now out of High School. was growing up rapidly; and anybody 'who knows anything at all about Branton Hills' history, knows that, if this band of bright, loyal pals of Gadsby's was out to attain a goal, it was mighty apt to start things humming, To say that Gadsby's rivals got a bad jolt as it got around town that his "bunch of warriors" was aiding him, would put it but mildly. *Two* quit *instantly,* saying that this is a day of Youth and no adult has half a show against it! But two still hung on; clinging to a sort of fond fantasy that Gadsby, not naturally a public sort of man, might voluntarily drop out. But, had Gadsby so much as thought of such an action, his Organization would quickly laugh it to scorn.

"Why, good gracious!" said Frank Morgan, "if *anybody* should sit in that Mayor's chair in City Hall, it's you! Just look at what you did to boost Branton Hills! Until you got it a-going it had but *two* thousand inhabitants; now it has sixty thousand! And just ask your rivals to point to any part of it that you didn't build up. Look at our Public Library, municipal band, occupational class rooms; auto and bus trips; and your

circus which paid for music for sick folks. With you as Mayor, *boy!*
What an opportunity to boss and swing things your own way! Why,
anything you might say is as good as law; and—"

"Now, hold on, boy!" said Gadsby, "a Mayor can't boss things in any
such a way as you think. A Mayor has a Council, which has to pass on
all bills brought up; and, my boy, upon arriving at manhood, you'll find
that a Mayor who *can* boss a Council around, is a most uncommon
bird. And as for a Mayor's word amounting to a law, it's a mighty good
thing that it can't! Why, a Mayor can't do much of anything, today,
Frank, without a bunch of crazy bat-brains stirring up a rumpus about
his acts looking 'suspiciously shady.' Now that is a bad condition in
which to find a city, Frank. You boy's don't know anything about graft;
but as you grow up you will find many flaws in a city's laws; but also
many points thoroughly good and fair. Just try to think what a city
would amount to if a solitary man could control its law making, as a
King or Sultan of old. That was why so many millions of inhabitants
would start wars and riots against a tyrant; for many a King *was* a tyrant, Frank, and had no thought as to how his laws would suit his thousands of rich and poor. A law that might suit a rich man, might work all
kinds of havoc with a poor family."

"But," said Frank. "why should a King pass a law that would dissat-
isfy anybody?"

Gadsby's parry to this rising youthful ambition for light on political
affairs was:—

"Why will a duck go into a pond?" and Frank found that though a
growing young man might know a thing or two, making laws for a city
was a man's job.

So, with a Mayoralty campaign on his hands, plus planning for that
big auditorium, Gadsby was as busy as a fly around a syrup jug; for a
mass of campaign mail had to go out; topics for orations thought up;
and contacts with his now truly important Organization of Youth, took
so many hours out of his days that his family hardly saw him, at all.
Noon naturally stood out as a good opportunity for oratory, as thousands, out for lunch, would stop, in passing. But, also, many a hall rang
with plaudits as an antagonist won a point; but many a throng saw
Gadsby's good points, and plainly told him so by turning out volumi-
nously at any point at which his oratory was to flow. It was truly miraculous how this man of shy disposition, found words in putting forth
his plans for improving Branton Hills, town of his birth. Many an ora-

tor has grown up from an unassuming individual who had things worth saying; and who, through that curious facility which is born of a conviction that his plans had a practical basis, won many a ballot against such prolific flows of high-sounding words as his antagonists had in stock. Many a night Gadsby was "all in," as his worn-out body and an aching throat sought his downy couch. No campaign is a cinch.

With so many minds amongst a city's population, just that many calls for this or that swung back and forth until that most important of all days,—voting day, was at hand. What crowds, mobs and jams did assail all polling booths casting ballots to land a party-man in City Hall! If a voting booth was in a school building, as is a common custom pupils had that day off; and, as Gadsby was Youth's champion, groups of kids hung around, watching and hoping with that avidity so common with youth, that Gadsby would win by a majority unknown in Branton Hills. And Gadsby did!

As soon as it was shown by official count, Branton Hills was a riot, from City Hall to City limits; throngs tramping around, tossing hats aloft; for a hard-working man had won what many thousands thought was fair and just.

AS SOON AS GADSBY'S inauguration had put him in a position to do things with authority, his first act was to start things moving on that big auditorium plan, for which many capitalists had bought bonds. Again public opinion had a lot to say as to how such a building should look, what it should contain; how long, how high, how costly; with a long string of ifs and buts.

Family upon family put forth claims for rooms for public forums in which various thoughts upon world affairs could find opportunity for discussion; Salvation Army officials thought that a big hall for a public Sunday School class would do a lot of good; and that, lastly, what I must, from this odd yarn's strict orthography, call a "film show," should, without doubt occupy a part of such a building. Anyway, talk or no talk, Gadsby said that it should stand as a building for man, woman and child; rich or poor; and, barring its "film show," without cost to anybody. Branton Hills' folks could thus swim, do gymnastics, talk on public affairs, or "just sit and gossip", at will. So it was finally built in a charming park amidst shrubs and blossoms; an additional honor for Gadsby.

But such buildings as Branton Hills now had could not fulfill all functions of so rapidly growing a city; for you find, occasionally, a class of folks who cannot afford a doctor, if ill. This was brought up by a girl of our Organization, Doris Johnson, who, on Christmas Day, in taking gifts to a poor family, had found a woman critically ill, and with no funds for aid or comforts; and instantly, in Doris' quick young mind a vision of a big city hospital took form; and, on a following day Gadsby had his Organization at City Hall, to "just talk," (and you *know* how that bunch *can* talk!) to a Councilman or two.

Now, if any kind of a building in all this big world costs good, hard cash to build, and furnish, it is a hospital; and it is also a building which a public knows nothing about. So Mayor Gadsby saw that if his Council would pass an appropriation for it, no such squabbling as had struck his Municipal Auditorium plan, would occur. But Gadsby forgot Branton Hills' landlords, all of whom had "a most glorious spot," just right for a hospital; until, finally, a group of physicians was told to look around. And did Branton Hills' landlords call upon Branton Hills' physicians? I'll say so!! Anybody visiting town, not knowing what was going on, would think that vacant land was as common as raindrops in a cloudburst. Small plots sprang into public light which couldn't hold a poultry barn, to say nothing of a big City Hospital. But no grasping landlord can fool physicians in talking up a hospital location, so it was finally built, on high land, with a charming vista across Branton Hills' suburbs and distant hills; amongst which Gadsby's charity auto and bus trips took so many happy invalids on past hot days.

Now it is only fair that our boys and girls of this famous Organization of Youth, should walk forward for an introduction to you. So I will bring forth such bright and loyal girls as Doris Johnson, Dorothy Fitts, Lucy Donaldson, Marian Hopkins, Priscilla Standish, Abigail Worthington, Sarah Young, and Virginia Adams. Among our boys, cast a fond look upon Arthur Rankin, Frank Morgan, John Hamilton, Paul Johnson, Oscar Knott and William Snow; as smart a bunch of Youth as you could find in a month of Sundays.

As soon as our big hospital was built and functioning, Sarah Young arid Priscilla Standish, in talking with groups of girls, had found a longing for a night-school, as so many folks had to work all day, so couldn't go to our Manual Training School. So Mayor Gadsby took it up with Branton Hills School Board. Now school boards do not always think in harmony with Mayors and Councils; in fact, what with school boards,

Councils, taxation boards, paving contractors, Sunday closing-hour agitations, railway rights of way, and all-round political "mud-slinging," a Mayor has a tough job.

Two of Gadsby's School Board said "NO! A right out-loud, slam-bang big "NO!!" Two thought that a night school was a good thing; but four, with a faint glow of financial wisdom, (a rarity in politics, today!) saw no cash in sight for such an institution.

But Gadsby's famous Organization won again! Branton Hills did not contain a family in which this Organization wasn't known; and many a sock was brought out from hiding, and many a sofa pillow cut into, to aid *any* plan in which this group had a part.

But, just as funds had grown to what Mayor Gadsby thought would fill all such wants, a row in Council as to this fund's application got so hot that "His Honor" got mad; mighty ,*mad!!* And said: "Why is it that any bill for appropriations coming up in this Council has to kick up such a rumpus? Why can't you look at such things with a public mind; for nothing can so aid toward passing bills as harmony. This city is not holding off an attacking army. Branton Hills is not a pack of wild animals, snapping and snarling by day; jumping, at *a* crackling twig, at night. It is a city of *humans;* animals, if you wish, but with a gift from On High of a *brain,* so far apart from all dumb animals as to allow us to talk about our public affairs calmly and thoughtfully. All this *Night* School rumpus is foolish. Naturally, what is taught in such a school is an important factor; so I want to find out from our Organization—"

At this point, old Bill Simpkins got up, with: "This Organization of Youth stuff puts a kink in my spinal column! Almost all of it is through school. So how can you bring such a group forward as 'pupils?' "

"A child," said Gadsby, "who had such schooling as Branton Hills affords is, naturally, still a pupil; for many will follow up a study if an opportunity is at hand. Many adults also carry out a custom of brushing up on unfamiliar topics; thus, also, ranking as pupils. Possibly, Bill, if you would look up that word 'pupil,' you wouldn't find so much fault with insignificant data."

"All right!" was Simpkins' snap-back; "but what I want to know is, what our big Public Library is for. Your 'pupils' can find all sorts of information in that big building. So why build a night school? It's nothing but a duplication!"

"A library," said Gadsby, is not a school. It has no instructors; you cannot talk in its rooms. You may find a book or two on your study, or you may not. You would find it a big handicap if you think that you can accomplish much with no aid but that of a Public Library. Young folks know what young folks want to study. It is foolish, say, to install a class in Astronomy, for although it *is* a 'Night School,' its pupils' thoughts might not turn toward Mars, Saturn or shooting stars; but shorthand, including training for typists amongst adults who, naturally don't go to day schools, is most important, today; also History and Corporation Law; and I know that a study of Music would attract many. Any man or woman who works all day, but still wants to study at night, should find an opportunity for doing so."

This put a stop to Councilman Simpkins' criticisms, and approval was put upon Gadsby's plan; and it was but shortly that this school's popularity was shown in a most amusing way. Branton Hills folks, in passing it on going out for a show or social call, caught most savory whiffs, as its cooking class was producing doughnuts and biscuits; for a Miss Chapman, long famous as a cook for Branton Hills' Woman's Club, had about forty girls finding out about that magic art. So, too, occasionally a cranky old Councilman, who had fought against "this foolish night school proposition," would pass by; and, oh, hum!! A Councilman is only an animal, you know; and, on cooking class nights, such an animal, unavoidably drawn by that wafting aroma, would go in, just a bit humiliatingly, and, in praising Miss Chapman for doing "such important work for our young girls," would avidly munch a piping hot biscuit or a sizzling doughnut from a young girl's hand, who, a month ago, couldn't fry a slab of bacon without burning it.

Just as Gadsby was thinking nothing was now lacking in Branton Hills, a child in a poor family got typhoid symptoms from drinking from a small brook at a picnic and, without any aid from our famous Organization, a public clamor was forthcoming for Municipal District Nursing, as so many folks look with horror at going to a hospital. Now District Nursing calls for no big appropriation; just salary, a first-aid outfit, a supply of drugs and so forth; and, now-a-days, a car. And, to Branton Hills' honor four girls who had had nursing training soon brought, not only small comforts, but important ministrations to a goodly part of our population. In districts without this important municipal function, common colds may run into long-drawn-out attacks; and contagion can not only shut up a school or two but badly handicap all forms of public activity.

"Too many small towns," said Gadsby, "try to go without public nursing; calling it foolish, and claiming that a family ought to look out for its own sick. BUT! Should a high mortality, such as, this Nation HAS known, occur again, such towns will frantically broadcast a call for girls with nursing training; and wish that a silly, cash-saving custom hadn't brought such critical conditions."

At this point I want to bring forward an individual who has had a big part in Branton Hills' growth; but who, up to now, has not shown up in this history. You know that Gadsby had a family, naturally including a woman; and that woman was fondly and popularly known throughout town as Lady Gadsby; a rank fittingly matching Gadsby's "His Honor," upon his inauguration as Mayor. Lady Gadsby was strongly in favor of all kinds of clubs or associations; organizing a most worthy Charity Club, a Book Club and a Political Auxiliary. It was but a natural growth from Woman's part in politics, both municipal and National; and which, in many a city, has had much to say toward nominations of good officials, and running many a crook out of town; for no crook, nor "gang boss" can hold out long if up against a strong Woman's Club. Though it was long thought that woman's brain was minor in comparison with man's, woman, as a class, now-a-day shows an all-round activity; and has brought staid control to official actions which had had a long run through domination by man;—that proud, cocky, strutting animal who thinks that this gigantic world should hop, skip and jump at his commands. So, from, or through just such clubs as Lady Gadsby's, Branton Hills was soon attracting folks from surrounding districts; in fact, it was known as a sort of Fairyland in which all things turn out satisfactorily. This *was,* plainly, a condition which would call for much additional building; which also brings additional tax inflow; so Branton Hills was rapidly growing into a most important community. So, at a School Board lunch, His Honor said:—"I trust that now you will admit that what I said long ago about making a city an attraction to tourists, is bringing daily confirmation. Oh, what a lot of politically blind city and town officials I could point out within a day's auto trip from Branton Hills! Many such an official, upon winning a foothold in City Hall, thinks only of his own cohorts, and his own gain. So it is not surprising that public affairs grow stagnant. Truly, I cannot fathom such minds! I can think of nothing so satisfying as doing public good in as many ways as an official can. Think, for an instant, as to just what a city is. As I said long ago, it is not an array of buildings, parks and fountains.

No. A city is a living thing! It is, actually, *human;* for it is a group of
humanity growing up in daily contact; and if officials adopt as a slogan,
"all I can do," and not "all I can grab," only its suburban boundary can
limit its growth. Branton Hills attracts thousands, annually. All of that
influx looks for comforts, an opportunity to work, and good schools.
Branton Hills has all that; and I want to say that all who visit us, with
thoughts of joining us, will find us holding out a glad hand; promising
that all such fond outlooks will find confirmation at any spot within
cannon-shot of City Hall."

At this point, a woman from just such a group got up, saying:—"I
want to back up your mayor. On my first visit to your charming city I
saw an opportunity for my family; and, with woman's famous ability
for arguing, I got my husband to think as I do; and not an hour from
that day has brought us any dissatisfaction. Your schools stand high in
comparison with any out our way; your shops carry first-class goods,
your laws act without favoritism for anybody or class; and an air of
happy-go-lucky conditions actually shouts at you, from all parts of
town."

Now, as months slid past it got around to Night School graduation
day; and as it was this institution's first, all Branton Hills was on hand,
packing its big hall. An important part was a musical half-hour by its
big chorus, singing such grand compositions as arias from Faust, Robin
Hood, Aida, and Martha; also both boys' and girls' bands, both brass
and strings, doing first-class work on a Sousa march, a Strauss waltz,
and a potpourri of National airs from many lands, which brought a
storm of hand clapping; for no form of study will so aid youth in living
happily, as music. Ability to play or sing; to know what is good or poor
in music, instills into young folks a high quality of thought; and, accu-
racy is found in its rigidity of rhythm.

As soon as this music class was through, Gadsby brought forth solo-
ists, duos and trios; violinists, pianists, and so many young musicians
that Branton Hills was as proud of its night school as a girl is of "that
first diamond." That brought our program around to introducing pupils
who had won honor marks: four girls in knitting, oil painting, cooking
and journalism; and four smart youths in brass work, wood-carving and
Corporation law. But pupils do not form all of a school body; so a
group of blushing instructors had to bow to an applauding roomful.

Though this was a school graduation, Mayor Gadsby said it would do no harm to point out a plan for still adding to Branton Hills' public spirit.

"This town is too plain; too dingy. Brick walls and asphalt paving do not light up a town, but dim it. So I want to plant all kinds of growing things along many of our curbs. In our parks I want ponds with gold fish, fancy ducks and big swans; row-boats, islands with arbors, and lots of shrubs *that blossom;* not just an array of twigs and stalks. I want, in our big City Park, a casino, dancing pavilion, lunch rooms; and parkings for as many cars as can crowd in. So I think that all of us ought to pitch in and put a bright array of natural aids round about; both in our shopping district and suburbs; for you know that old saying, that 'a charming thing is a joy always.' "

So a miraculous transformation of any spot at all dull was soon a fact. Oak, birch and poplar saplings stood along curbs and around railway stations; girls brought in willow twigs, ivy roots, bulbs of canna, dahlia, calladium, tulip, jonquil, gladiola and hyacinth. Boys also dug many woodland shrubs which, standing along railway tracks, out of town, took away that gloomy vista so commonly found upon approaching a big city; and a long grassplot, with a rim of boxwood shrubs, was laid out, half way from curb to curb on Broadway, in Branton Hills' financial district. As Gadsby was looking at all this with happy satisfaction, a bright lad from our Night School's radio class, told him that Branton Hills should install a broadcasting station, as no city, today, would think of trying to win additional population without that most important adjunct for obtaining publicity. So any man or boy who had any knack at radio was all agog; and about a thousand had ambitions for a job in it, at which only about six can work. And City Hall had almost a riot, as groups of politicians, pastors and clubs told just what such a station should, and should not broadcast; for a broadcasting station, with its vast opportunity for causing both satisfaction and antagonism, must hold rigidly aloof from any racial favoritism, church, financial or nationality criticisms; and such a policy is, as any broadcasting station will admit, most difficult of adoption. First of all stood that important position of what you might call "studio boss." Although a man in control of a station is not known as "boss," I think it will pass in this oddly built-up story. Now I am going to boost our famous Organization again, by stating that a boy from its ranks, Frank Morgan, was put in; for it was a hobby of Gadsby to put Branton Hills boys in Branton Hills municipal jobs. So Frank, right away, got all sorts of calls for hours or half hours to broadcast "most astounding bargains in clothing, salad oils, motor oils, motor "gas", soaps, cars, and tooth brush lubricants.

With a big Fall campaign for Washington officials about to start, such a position as Frank's was chuck full of pitfalls; a stiff proposition for a young chap, not long out of High School. But Gadsby took him in hand.

"Now, boy, hold your chin up, and you will find that most folks, though cranky or stubborn at first, will follow your rulings if you insist, in a civil way, that you know all our National Radio Commission's laws binding your station. *Millions,* of all kinds, will dial in your station; and what would highly satisfy a group in Colorado might actually insult a man down in Florida; for radio's wings carry far. You know I'll back you up, boy. But now, what would you call this station?"

"Oh," said our tyro-boss; a radio station should work with initials showing its location. So a Branton Hills station could stand as KBH."

Such initials, ringing with civic patriotism, hit Gadsby just right; his Council put it in writing; and "Station KBH" was born! Though it is not important to follow it from now on, I will say that our vast country, by tuning in on KBH, found out a lot about this Utopia.

"You know that good old yarn," said Gadsby, "about making so good a rat-trap that millions will tramp down your grass in making a path to your front door."

Now don't think that our famous Organization, having shown its worth on so many occasions, sat down without thinking of doing anything again. No, sir! Not *this* bunch! If a boy or girl thought of any addition to Branton Hills' popularity it was brought to Mayor Gadsby for consultation. And so, as Lucy Donaldson on a trip through a patch of woods, *saw* a big stag looking out from a clump of shrubs, nothing would do but to rush to His Honor to pour what thoughts that charming sight had brought up in this bright young mind. So, as Gadsby stood at City Hall's front door, this palpitating, gushing young girl ran towards him, panting and blowing from a long run.

"I want a zoo!

"A WHAT?"

"A ZOO!! *You* know! A park with stags and all kinds of wild animals; and a duck pond, and—and—and—"

"Whoa! Slow down a bit! Do you want an actual zoo, or an outfit of toys that wind up and growl?"

"I want a truly, out-and-out, big zoo. Why can't you build walls around a part of City Park, and—"

Gadsby saw that this was an addition which nobody had thought of, until now; so, grasping his young visitor's hand, joyfully, said:—

"It's a fact, Lucy!! And, as you thought of it, I'll call it,—now wait;—what *shall* I call it? Aha! That's it! I'll call it 'Lucy Zoo'. How's that for quick thinking?"

"My! That's just grand; but what will Papa say?"

Now Gadsby had known Lucy's family from boyhood, so said:— "You inform your dad that at any sign of balking by him, I'll put HIM in Lucy Zoo, and pay a boy to prod him with a sharp stick, until his approval is in my hands." This brought such a rollicking laugh that a man mowing City Hall lawn had to laugh, too.

Now, (Ah! But I can't avoid saying it!) our Organization was out again; but, now having grown a bit from such childish youths as had, at first stood in its ranks, a boy, now approaching manhood, and a girl, now a young woman, could solicit funds with an ability to talk knowingly in favor of any factor that a hanging-back contributor could bring up in running down such a proposition. You can always count on finding that class in any city or town upon any occasion for public works; but I can proudly say that many saw good in our Organization's plan; and Lucy soon found that out, in Old Lady Flanagan.

"Whoops! A zoo, is it? And pray, phwat can't thot crazy Gadsby think up? If our big Mayor had four sich bys as I brought into this woild; worra, worra! his parlor, halls, dinin' room an back yard'd furnish him wid a zoo, all right! Wid two always a-scrappin' about a ball bat or a sling shot; a brat continually a-bawlin' about nuthin'; an' a baby wid whoopin' cough, *I* know phwat a zoo is, widout goin' to City Park to gawk at a indigo baboon, or a pink tom cat."

"But," said Lucy, trying hard not to laugh; "Mayor Gadsby isn't thinking of putting in pink tom cats, nor any kind of tom cats in this zoo. It is for only *wild* animals."

"WILD!! Say, if you could look into my back door as Old Man Flanagan quits work, an brings back a load o' grog, you'd find thot you had wild animals roight in this town, all roight, all roight."

But, as on so many occasions, this charming girl got a contribution, with Old Lady Flanagan calling out from a front window:—

"Good luck, Lucy darlin'! I'm sorry I was so dom cranky!"

But though popular opinion was in favor of having a zoo, popular opinion didn't hand in donations to within four thousand dollars of what it would cost to install; and Gadsby and his "gang" had to do a bit of brain racking, so as not to disappoint lots of good folks who *had* paid in. Finally, Sarah Young thought of a rich woman living just across from City Park. This woman, Lady Standish, was of that kind, loving disposition which would bring in a cold, hungry, lost pup, or cat, and fill it up with hot food and milk. Branton Hills kids could bring any kind of a hurt or sick animal or bird; and Sarah had long known that that back yard was, actually, a small zoo, anyway; with dogs, cats, poultry, two robins too young to fly, four sparrows and a canary, almost bald. Sarah thought that any woman, loving animals as Lady Standish did, might just thrill at having a big zoo-ful right at hand. So, saying, "I'll go and find out, right now", was off as an arrow from a bow. As soon as this kindly woman found out what was on Sarah's mind, our young solicitor got a loving kiss, with:—"A zoo! Oh! how truly charming! What *grand* things Mayor Gadsby can think up without half trying!" And Sarah had to grin, thinking of Lucy, and Old Lady Flanagan's opinion of His Honor! "You may not know it, Sarah," said Lady Standish, "but John Gadsby and I had a big flirtation, way back in our school days. And HOW downcast poor Johnny was at my finding a husband out of town! But that was long, long ago, darling. So, just to sort of pacify my old pal, John, I'll gladly put up your missing four thousand; and you go to His Honor and say that I wish him all sorts of good luck with this plan."

Now, Olympic champions must train continuously, but, customarily, in gymnasiums. But today, folks in Branton Hills' shopping district had to turn and gasp; for a young woman was sprinting wildly toward City Hall; for Sarah was in a hurry. Gadsby was just coming out, as this girl, as badly blown as Lucy was in asking for a zoo, ran up, calling out:—"I GOT IT!! I GOT IT!!"

"Got what? A fit?"

"No! I got that final four thousand dollars! It's from Lady Standish, who says that way back in school days, you and—"

"Whoa!! That was back in *history?*" but Gadsby was blushing, and Sarah was winking, coyly.

Now Gadsby was as fond of his Organization boys and girls as of his own; and Sarah was so radiantly happy that all His Honor could say was:—

"My, now, Sarah! That's mighty good work! And as I told Lucy I'd call our zoo Lucy Zoo for thinking of it, I'll find a *way* to honor you, too. Aha! I'll put up a big arch, through which all visitors must pass, and call it 'Sarah Young's Rainbow Arch.' How's that?"

Now Sarah had a bit of natural wit; so quickly said:—

"That's just grand if you'll bury that famous pot of gold at its foot, so I can dig it up!"

NOW THAT A Zoo was actually on its way, Gadsby had to call in various groups to talk about what a Zoo should contain. Now, you know that *all* animals can't find room in this orthographically odd story; so, if you visit Lucy Zoo, you'll miss a customary inhabitant, or two. But you'll find an array worthy of your trip. So a call was put in two big daily journals, asking for bids on animals and birds; and soon, from north, south and criss-cross points, a hunting party or a city with too many zoo animals on hand got in touch with Branton Hills, with proposals for all kinds of animals, from kangaroos to bats; and our Organization had a lot of fun planning how many it could crowd into City Park, without crowding out visitors. Finally a ballot put Lucy's zoological population as follows:—

First, according to Lucy, "an awfully, AWFULLY big hippopotamus, with a pool for its comfort;" a yak, caribou, walrus, (also with a pool,) a long fox-run, bison, gnus, stags, (it was a stag, you know, that got this zoo plan going!), alligators, mountain lions, African lions, wild cats, wild boars, llamas, gorillas, baboons, orang-outangs, mandrills; *and,* according to Gadsby's boys, a "big gang" of that amusing, tiny mimic always found accompanying hand-organs. Also an aviary, containing condors, buzzards, parrots, ibis, macaws, adjutant birds, storks, owls, quail, falcons, tiny humming birds, a sprinkling of hawks, mocking birds, swans, fancy ducks, toucans; and a host of small singing birds; and oh! without fail, an ostrich family; and, last, but most important of all, a big first cousin of old Jumbo! A big glass building would hold boa constrictors, pythons, cobras, lizards, and so forth; and down in back of all this, an outdoor aquarium, full of goldfish, rainbow trout, various fancy fish and blossoming aquatic plants. All in all it would furnish a mighty amusing and popular spot which would draw lots of out-of-town visitors; and visitors, you know, *might* turn into inhabitants! And so things finally got around to Inauguration Day; and, knowing that no kid could sit still in school on such an occasion, it was put down for a Saturday; and, so many happy, shouting, hopping, jumping kids stood waiting for His Honor to cut a satin ribbon in front of Sarah Young's Rainbow Arch, that grown folks had to wait, four blocks back. As Gadsby was roaming around with Lucy, to find if things should start moving, old Pat Ryan, from Branton Hills' railway station, was hunting for him; finally locating him in a lunch room, and rushing in with:——

"Say! That big hop-skip-and-jump artist is down in my trunk room! I got a punch on my jaw, a crack on my snout, and a kick on my shins a-tryin' to calm him down!"

"A kick and a punch? What actions!" said Gadsby. "I don't know of any hop-skip-and-jump artist. How big a man is it?"

"Worra, worra! It ain't no man at all, at all! It's that thing what grows in Australia, and——"

But Lucy saw light right off; and "laughing fit to kill," said

"Oh, ho, ho!! *I* know! It's that boxing kangaroo you bought from Barnum's circus!" and a charming girl was doubling up in a wild storm of giggling, ignoring old Pat's scowls.

"Ah! That's him, all right," said Gadsby. "So, Pat, just put him in a burlap bag and ship him to this zoo.

"Who? *I* put him in a burlap bag? Say, boss! If I can pick up about six husky guys around that station; and if I can find a *canvas,* not a burlap, bag; and put on a gas mask, a stomach pad, two shin-guards, and——"

But that crowd at Sarah's Arch was shouting for Gadsby to cut that ribbon so old Pat had to bag that Australian tornado; and in a way that would not hurt him; for kangaroo actors cost good cash, you know.

So that crowd of kids got in, at last! Now zoo animals can think, just as humans can; and it was amusing to watch a pair of boys staring at a pair of orang-outangs; and a pair of orang-outangs staring back at a pair of boys; both thinking, no doubt, what funny things it saw! And, occasionally, both animal and boy won a point! Now if you think that only young folks find any fun in going to a zoo, you probably don't go to zoos much; for many a big, rotund capitalist had to laugh at simian antics, though, probably figuring up just how much satisfaction his cash contribution brought him. Many a family woman forgot such things as a finicky child or burning biscuits. All was happy-go-lucky joy; and, at two o'clock, as Branton Hills' Municipal Band, (a part of Gadsby's Organization of Youth's work, you know) struck up a bright march, not a glum physiognomy was found in all that big park.

Gadsby and Lucy had much curiosity in watching what such crashing music would do to various animals. At first a spirit akin to worry had baboons, gorillas, and such, staring about, as still as so many posts; until, finding that no harm was coming from such sounds, soon took to climbing and swinging again. Stags, yaks and llamas did a bit of high-kicking at first; Gadsby figuring that drums, and not actual music, did it. But a lilting waltzing aria did not worry any part of this big zoo family; in fact, a fox, wolf and jackal, in a quandary at first actually lay down, as though music truly "hath charms to calm a wild bosom."

At Gadsby's big aquarium visitors found not only fun, but opportunity for studying many a kind of fish not ordinarily found in frying pans; and, though in many lands, snails form a popular food, Lucy, Sarah and Virginia put on furious scowls at a group of boys who thought "Snails might go good, with a nut—pick handy." (But boys always *will* say things to horrify girls, you *know.)* And upon coming to that big glass building, with its boa constrictors, alligators, lizards and so on, a boy grinningly "got a girl's goat" by wanting to kiss a fifty-foot anaconda; causing Lucy to say, haughtily, that "No boy, wanting to kiss such horrid, wriggly things can kiss us Branton Hills girls." (Good for you, Lucy! I'd pass up a *sixty-foot* anaconda, any day, for *you.)*

In following months many a school class was shown through our zoo's fascinating paths, as instructors told of this or that animal's habits and natural haunts; and showing that it was as worthy of sympathy, if ill, as any human. And not only did such pupils obtain kindly thoughts for zoo animals, but cats, dogs and all kinds of farm stock soon found that things had an uncommon look, through a dropping off in scoldings and whippings, and rapidly improving living conditions. But most important of all was word from an ugly, hard-looking woman, who, watching, with an apologizing sniff, a flock of happy birds, said:—

"I'm sorry that I always slap and bawl out my kids so much, for I know, now, that kids or animals won't do as you wish if you snap and growl too much. And I trust that Mayor Gadsby knows what a lot of good all his public works do for us."

Now this is a most satisfactory and important thing to think about, for brutality will not, cannot,—accomplish what a kindly disposition will; and, if folks could only know how quickly a "balky" child will, through loving and cuddling, grow into a charming, happy youth, much childish gloom and sorrow would vanish; for a man or woman who is ugly to a child is too low to rank as highly as a wild animal; for no animal will stand, for an instant, anything approaching an attack, or any form of harm to its young. But what a lot of tots find slaps, yanks and hard words for conditions which do not call for such harsh tactics! *No* child is naturally ugly or "cranky." And big, gulping sobs, or sad, unhappy young minds, in a tiny body should *not* occur in any community of civilization. Adulthood holds many an opportunity for such conditions. Childhood should not.

Now just a word about zoos. Many folks think that animals in a zoo know no comforts; nothing but constant fright from living in captivity. Such folks do not stop to think of a thing or two about an animal's wild condition. Wild animals must not only constantly hunt for food, but invariably fight to kill it and to *hold* it, too; for, in such a fight, a big antagonist will naturally win from a small individual. Thus, what food is found, is also lost; and hunting must go on, day by day, or night by night until a tragic climax—by thirst or starvation. But in a zoo, food is brought daily, with facility for drinking, and laid right in front of hoofs, paws or bills. For small animals, roofs and thick walls ward off cold winds and rain; and so, days of calm inactivity, daily naps without worrying about attack; and a carting away of all rubbish and filth soon puts a zoo animal in bodily form which has no comparison with its wild condition. Lack of room in which to climb, roam or play, *may* bring a zoo animal to that condition known as "soft"; but, as it now has no call for vigor, and its fighting passions find no opportunity for display, such an animal is gradually approaching that condition which has brought Man, who is only an animal, anyway, to his lofty point in Natural History, today. Truly, with such tribulations, worry, and hard work as Man puts up with to obtain his food and lodging, a zoo animal, if it could only know of our daily grind, would comfortably yawn, thankful that Man is so kindly looking out for it. With similar animals all around it, and, day by day, just a happy growth from cub-hood to maturity, I almost wish that I was a zoo animal, with no boss to growl about my not showing up, mornings, at a customary hour!

Now, as our Organization of Youth is rapidly growing up, a *young* crowd, too young to join it at first, is coming up; imbibing its "why-not-do-it-now?" spirit. So, as Gadsby stood in front of that big Municipal Auditorium (which that group, you know, had had built), Marian Hopkins, a small girl, in passing by, saw him, and said, "I think Branton Hills ought to buy a balloon."

"Balloon? Balloon? What would this city do with a balloon? Put a string on it so you could run around with it?"

"No, not that kind of a balloon, but that big, zooming kind that sails way up high, with a man in it."

"Oh! Ha, ha! You think an aircraft is a balloon! But what would— Aha! An airport?"

"Uh—huh; but I didn't know how to say it."

"It's cracky!" said His Honor. "I thought this town was about through improving. But an airport *would* add a bit to it; now wouldn't it?"

Marian had a most profound opinion that it *would;* (if profound opinions grow in such small kids!) so both took a walk to City Hall to hunt up a Councilman or two. Finding four in a Council room, Gadsby said, "Youth, or, I should say, childhood, has just shown that Branton Hills is shy on a most important acquisition," and Old Bill Simpkins just *had* to blurt out:—"And, naturally, it calls for cash! CASH!

CASH! CASH!! What will this town amount to if it blows in dollars so fast?"

"And," said Gadsby, "what will it amount to, if it don't?"

That put a gag on Old Bill. Councilman Banks, though, was curious to know about Marian's proposition, saying:—"It is probably a plan for buying Christmas toys for all Branton Hills kids."

But tiny Marian, with a vigorous stamp of a tiny foot, swung right back with:—"NO, SIR!! Santa Claus will bring us our gifts! But I thought of having a—what did you call it, Mayor Gadsby?"

"This child thinks Branton Hills should build an airport, and I think so, too. If our inhabitants, such as this tot, can think up such things, all adults should pack up, and vanish from municipal affairs. All right, Marian; our City Council, *your* City Council, my young patriot, will look into this airport plan for you."

So, as on similar occasions months ago, word that land was again cropping up in Gadsby's mind, brought out a flood of landlords with vacant lots, all looking forward to disposing of a dump worth two dollars and a half, for fifty thousand. Now an airport must occupy a vast lot of land, so cannot stand right in a City's shopping district; but finally a big tract was bought, and right in back of tiny Marian's back yard! Instantly, City Hall was full of applicants for flying Branton Hills' first aircraft. To Gadsby's joy, amongst that bunch was Harold Thompson, an old Organization lad, who was known around town as a chap who could do about anything calling for brains. As an airport is not laid out in a day, Harold got busy with paid aviators and soon was piloting a craft without aid; and not only Branton Hills folks, but old aviators, saw in Harold, a "bird-man" of no small ability. And so tiny Marian's "vision" was a fact; just as "big girl" Lucy's Zoo; and, as with all big City affairs, an Inauguration should start it off. Now, on all such affairs you always find a "visitor of honor"; and on this grand day Gadsby couldn't think of anybody for that important post but Marian. And, as it would occur in August, any day would do, as that is a school vacation month.

And what a *mob* stood, or sat, on that big airport, waiting for a signal from young Marian which would start Harold aloft, on Branton Hills' initial flight! Almost all brought a lunch and camp-stools or folding chairs; and, as it was a hot day, thousands of gay parasols, and an array of bright clothing on our school-girls, had that big lot looking as brilliant as a florist's window at Christmas.

Our young visitor of honor was all agog with joy; and, I think, possibly a touch of vanity; for what child *wouldn't* thrill with thousands watching? But though Marian had always had good clothing, coming from a family who could afford it, *no* tot, in all history, had so glorious an outfit as that which about all Branton Hills' population saw on that platform, amidst flags, bunting and our big Municipal Band. As an airship is a simulation of a bird; and as a bird, to a child, is not far from a fairy, Marian had gaudy fairy wings, a radiant cloak of gold, a sparkling gown all aglow with twinkling stars, and a long glass wand, with a star at its top. As soon as all was in condition Gadsby told Marian to stand up. This brought that vast crowd up, also; and Gadsby said:—

"Now hold your wand way up high, and swing it, to signal Harold to start."

Up shot a tiny arm; and Harold, watching from his cockpit, sang out:—

"CONTACT!!"

A vigorous twist of his ship's gigantic "fan", a shout, a roar, a whizz, a mighty cloud of dust, and amid a tornado of clapping, shouts, and band music, Branton Hills was put on aviation's map. Way, way up, so far as to look as small as a toy, Harold put on a show of banking, rolling and diving, which told Gadsby that, still again, had Branton Hills found profit in what its Organization of Youth, *and, now, its small kids,* had to say about improving a *town.*

During that box-lunch picnic, many of our "big girls" brought so much food to Marian that Dad and Ma had to stand guard against tummy pains. And what a glorious, jolly occasion that picnic was! Gay band music, songs, dancing, oratory; and a grand all-round "howdy" amongst old inhabitants and arriving tourists soon was transforming that big crowd into a happy group, such as it is hard to find, today, in any big city: cold, distant, and with no thought by its politicians for anybody in it; and Gadsby found, around that big airport, many a man, woman and child who was as proud of him as was his own family.

I THINK THAT now you should know this charming Gadsby family; so I will bring forth Lady Gadsby, about whom I told you at Gadsby's inauguration as Mayor; a loyal church woman with a vocal ability for choir work; and, with good capability on piano or organ, no woman could "fill in" in so many ways; and no woman was so willing, and quick to do so. Gadsby had two sons; bright lads and popular with all. Julius was of a studious turn of mind, always poring through books of information; caring not what kind of information it was, so long as it was information, and not fiction. Gadsby had thought of his growing up as a school instructor, for no work is so worthy as imparting what you know to any who long to study. But William! Oh, hum!! Our Mayor and Lady Gadsby didn't know just *what* to do with him; for all his thoughts clung around girls and fashions in clothing: Probably our High School didn't contain a girl who didn't think that, at no distant day, Bill Gadsby would turn, from a callow youth, into a "big catch" husband; for a Mayor's son in so important a city as ours was a mark for any girl to shoot at. But Bill was not of a marrying disposition; loving girls just *as* girls, but holding out no hand to any in particular. Always in first class togs, without missing a solitary fad which a young man should adopt, Gadsby's Bill was a lion, in his own right, with no girl in sight who had that tact through which a lasso could land around his manly throat. Gadsby had many a laugh, looking back at his own boyhood days, his various flirtations, and such wild, throbbing palpitations as a boy's flirtations can instill; and looking back through just such ogling groups as now sought his offspring; until a girl, oh, *so* long ago, had put a stop to all such flirtations, and got that lasso on "with a strangling hold," as Gadsby says; and it is still on, today! But this family was not all boys. Oh, my, no! Two girls also sat around that family board. First, following William, was Nancy, who, as Gadsby laughingly said, "didn't know how to grow;" and now, in High School, was "about as big as a pint of milk;" and of such outstanding charm that Gadsby continually got solicitations to allow photographing for soft-drink and similar billboard displays.

"No, sir!! Not for any sort of pay!! In allowing public distribution of a girl's photo you don't know into what situations said photos will land. I find, daily, photographs of girls blowing about vacant lots, all soggy from rains; also in a ditch, with its customary filth; or stuck up on a brick wall or drawn onto an imaginary body showing a brand of tights or pajamas. *No, sir!!* Not for *my* girl!!"

Fourth in this popular family was Kathlyn, of what is known as a "classical mold;" with a brain which, at no distant day, will rank high in Biology and Microscopy; for Kathlyn was of that sort which finds fascination in studying out many whats and whys amongst that vast array of facts about our origin. This study, which too many young folks avoid as not having practical worth had a strong hold on Kathlyn, who could not sanction such frivolous occupations as cards, dancing, or plain school gossip. Not for an instant! Kathlyn thought that such folks had no thoughts for anything but transitory thrills. But in Biology!! Ah!! Why not study it, and find out how a tiny, microscopic drop of protoplasm, can, through unknown laws grow into living organisms, which can not only go on living, but can also bring forth offspring of its kind? And not only that. As said offspring must combat various kinds of surroundings and try various foods, why not watch odd variations occur, and follow along, until you find an animal, bird, plant or bug of such a total dissimilarity as to form practically, a class actually apart from its original form? Kathlyn did just that; and Gadsby was proud of it; and, I think, just a bit curious on his own part as to occasional illustrations in this studious young lady's school books!

Now it is known by all such natural "faddists" that any such a study has points in common with a branch akin to it; and Kathlyn was not long in finding out that Biology, with its facts of animal origin, could apply to a practical control of bugs on farms. (This word, "bugs," is hardly Biological; but as Kathlyn is in this story, with its strict orthographical taboo, "bugs" must unavoidably supplant any classical nomination for such things.)

So, Mayor Gadsby sought Branton Hills' Council's approval for a goodly sum; not only for such control, but also for study as to how to plant, in ordinary soil, and not risk losing half a crop from worms, slugs and our awkwardly-brought-in "bugs." This appropriation was a sort of prod, showing this Council that publicity of any first-class kind was good for a city; and was casting about for anything which would so act, until Gadsby's son, Bill, (who, you know, thought of nothing but girls and "dolling up,") found that Branton Hills had no distinction of its own in outfits for man or woman, so why not put up a goal of, say fifty dollars, for anybody who could think up any worthy "stunt" in clothing; which should go out as "Branton Hills' This" or "Branton Hills' That." Possibly just a form of hat-brim, a cut of coat-front, or a sporting outfit. And our worthy Council did put up that goal, and many brought all sorts of plans to City Hall. And Bill won, by thinking up a girls' (always girls, with Bill!) hiking outfit, consisting of a skirt with a rain-proof lining, which could, during a storm, form a rain-suit by putting it on, as Bill said, "by substituting outwards for inwards." (This will hit Bill amusingly, as days go by!) Going with it was a shirt with a similar "turn—out" facility, and a hiking boot with high tops as guards against thorns and burs; but which, by undoing a clasp, would slip off; and, LO!! you had a low-cut Oxford for ordinary occasions! In about a month a big cotton mill had work going full blast on "Branton Hills' Turn-it-out Sport and Hiking Outfit," and a small boot-shop got out a pair of Bill's "two-part boots," though saying that it would "probably fall apart without warning!" But Kathlyn put on a pair and found it most satisfactory for a long, rough hill-climb, hunting for bird and animal forms for Biological study. This proof of Branton Hills' goods was soon known in surrounding towns, and that critical boot-shop and big cotton mill had hard work to fill calls from Canada, Holland, Russia, Spain and Australia! And Bill was put upon Branton Hills' Roll of Honor.

Now I'll drop civic affairs for a bit, and go on to a most natural act in this city of many young chaps and charming young girls which was slowly working up all through this history, as Mayor Gadsby had occasion to find out, sitting comfortably on his porch on a hot, sultry August night. Amidst blossoming shrubs, a dim form slowly trod up his winding pathway. It was a young man, plainly trying to act calmly, but couldn't. It was Frank Morgan, our radio broadcasting "boss", you know, who, for many a month, had shown what a romantic public calls "a crush" for Gadsby's young Nancy.

So a jolly call of:—"What's on your mind, boy?" rang out, as Frank sank willingly into a hammock, wiping his brow of what I *actually* know was *not* natural humidity from an August night! Now Gadsby, who was, as I said, a gay Lothario in his own youth, saw right off what was coming, and sat back, waiting. Finally, finishing a bad attack of coughing, (though Frank hadn't any cold!), that young man said:— "I,—that is, Nancy and I,—or, I will say that I want to,—that is,—I think Nancy and I would—" and Gadsby took pity on him, right off.

Nancy had always had a strong liking for Frank. Both had grown up in Branton Hills from babyhood; and Gadsby thought back about that lassoo which had brought him Lady Gadsby. Now asking a girl's Dad for that young lady's hand is no snap for any young swain; and Gadsby was just that kind of a Dad who would smooth out any bumps or rough spots in such a young swain's path. Nancy wasn't a child, now, but a grown-up young woman: so Gadsby said:—"Frank, Lady Gadsby and I know all about how much you think of Nancy; and what Nancy thinks of you. So, if you want to marry, our full wish is for a long and happy union. Nancy is out in that arbor, down this back path; and I'll watch that nobody disturbs you two for an hour."

At this grand turn of affairs, Frank could only gasp:—"OH—H—H!!' and a shadowy form shot down that dusky path; and from that moonlit arbor, anybody knowing how a man chirps to a canary bird, would know that two young birds put a binding approval upon what His Honor had just said!!

Many a man has known that startling instant in which Dan Cupid, that busy young rascal, took things in hand, and told him that his baby girl was not a baby girl now, and was about to fly away from him. It is both a happy and a sad thrill that shoots through a man at such an instant. Happy and joyous at his girl's arrival at maturity; sad, as it brings to mind that awkward fact that his own youth is now but a myth; and that his scalp is showing vacant spots. His baby girl in a bridal gown! His baby girl a Matron! His baby girl proudly placing *a grandchild* in his lap!! It's an impossibility!! But this big world is full of this kind of impossibility, and will stay so as long as Man lasts.

So Nancy, tiny, happy, laughing Nancy, was "found" through a conspiracy by Dan Cupid and Frank Morgan; and right in all glory of youth. *Youth!!* Ah, what a word!! And how transitory! But, how grand! as long as it lasts. How many millions in gold would pour out for an ability to call it all back, as with our musical myth, Faust. During that magic part of a child's growth this world is just a gigantic inquiry box, containing many a topic for which a solution is paramount to a growing mind. And to whom can a child look, but us adults? Any man who "can't stop now" to talk with a child upon a topic which, to him is "too silly for anything," should look back to that day upon which *that* topic was dark and dubious in his own brain. A child who asks nothing will know nothing. That is why that "bump of inquiry" was put on top of our skulls.

BUT TO GO BACK to Nancy. It was in August that Frank had stumblingly told Gadsby of his troth; and so, along in April, Branton Hills was told that a grand church ritual would occur in May. May, with its blossoms, birds and balmy air! An idyllic month for matrimony. I wish that I could call this grand church affair by its common, customary nomination; but that word can't possibly crowd into *this* story. It must pass simply as a church ritual.

All right; so far, so good. So, along into April all Branton Hills was agog, awaiting information as to that actual day; or, I should say, night.

Gadsby's old Organization of Youth was still as loyal to all in it as it was, way back in days of its formation; days of almost constantly running around town, soliciting funds for many a good Municipal activity. Finally this group got cards announcing that on May Fourth, Branton Hills' First Church would admit all who might wish to aid in starting Nancy and Frank upon that glamorous path to matrimonial bliss.

May Fourth was punctual in arriving; though many a young girl got into that flighty condition in which a month drags along as though in irons, and clock-hands look as if stuck fast. But to many girls, also, May Fourth was not any too far away; for charming gowns and dainty hats do not grow upon shrubs, you know; and girls who work all day must hurry at night, at manipulating a thousand or so things which go towards adorning our girls of today.

Now, an approach to a young girl's "big day" is not always as that girl might wish. Small things bob up, which, at first, look actually disastrous for a joyous occasion; and for Nancy and Frank, just such a thing did bob up; for, on May Third, a pouring rain and whistling wind put Branton Hills' spirits way, way down into a sorrowful slump. Black, ugly, rumbling clouds hung aggravatingly about in a saturation of mist, rain and fog; and roads and lawns got such a washing that Nancy said:—"Anyway, if I can't *walk* across that front church yard, I can *swim* it!!"

That was Nancy; a small bunch of inborn good humor; and I'll say, right now, that it *took* good humor, and lots of it, to look upon conditions out of your control, with such outstanding pluck!

But young Dan Cupid was still around, and got in touch with that tyrannical mythological god who controls storms; and put forth such a convincing account of all Nancy's good points, (and Frank's too, if anybody should ask you) that a command rang out across a stormy sky:—"Calling all clouds!! Calling all clouds!! All rain to stop at midnight of May Third! Bright Sun on May Fourth, and no wind!"

So, as Nancy took an anxious squint out of doors at about six o'clock on that important morning, (and what young girl *could* go on, calmly snoozing on such a day?) Lo!! Old Sol was smiling brightly down on Branton Hills; birds sang; all sorts of blossoming things had had a good drink; and a most *glorious* sky, rid of all ugly clouds, put our young lady into such a happy mood that it took a lot of control to avoid just a tiny bit of humidity around a small pair of rich, brown orbs which always had that vibrating, dancing light of happy youth; that miraculous "joy of living."

And, *what* a circus was soon going full tilt in Mayor Gadsby's mansion! If that happy man so much as said:—

"Now, I—" a grand, womanly chorus told him that "a man don't know anything about such affairs;" and that a most satisfactory spot for him was in a hammock on his porch, with a good cigar! That's it! A man is nominally monarch in his own family; but *only* so on that outstanding day upon which a bridal gown is laid out in all its glory on his parlor sofa, and a small mob of girls, and occasionally a woman or two, is rushing in and out, up and down stairs, and finding as much to do as a commonly known microscopic "bug" of prodigious hopping ability finds at a dog show. *Rush! rush! rush!* A thousand thoughts and a million words, (this crowd was all girls, you know!) making that parlor as noisy as a saw mill! But Gadsby laughingly staid out of it all, watching big armfuls of bloom and many a curious looking box go in through that front door; flying hands rapidly untying glorious ribbon wrappings.

Now, upon all such occasions you will find, if you snoop around in dining room or pantry, an astonishing loaf of culinary art, all fancy frosting, and chuck full of raisins and citron, which is always cut upon such an auspicious occasion; and it is as hard to avoid naming it, in this story, as it is to withstand its assault upon your stomach.

Oh hum! Now what? Aha! May Fourth, lasting, as Nancy said, "for about a million months," finally got Gadsby's dining room clock around to six-fifty; only about an hour, now, to that grand march past practically half of Branton Hills' population; for all who couldn't jam into that commodious church would stand around in a solid phalanx, blocking all traffic in that part of town; for all Branton Hills was fond of its Mayor's "baby girl."

But, during this rush and hubbub, how about Frank? Poor boy! Now, if you think that a young lad at such an instant is as calm as a millpond, you don't know romantic Youth, that's all. About forty of Gadsby's old Organization boys, now many young chaps, had bought him a car, which Nancy was *not* to know anything about until that throwing of old boots, and what is also customary, had quit. Frank didn't want to hold it back from Nancy, but what can a chap do, against forty? Also, last night, at a big "so sorry, old chap" party, Frank had found how loyal a bunch of old pals can turn out; and this "grand launching into matrimonial doubt" had put him in a happy mood for that all important oration of two words :—

"I do."

So now I'll hurry around to church to find out how Nancy's Organization girls put in a long day of hard labor; not only at floor work, but up on stools and chairs. My! My! Just *look* and gasp!! A long chain of lilacs runs from door to altar in two rows. And *look at* that big arch of wistaria and narcissus half way along! Artificial palms stand in curving ranks from organ to walls; and, with all lights softly glowing through pink silk hoods; and with gilt cords outlining an altar-dais of moss and sprays of asparagus, it is a sight to bring a thrill to anybody, young or old.

And, *now—aha!!* With organist and Pastor waiting, a murmur and hand-clapping from that big front door told all who had luckily got in that Nancy was coming! It took thirty cars to bring that bridal party to church; for not a boy or girl of our old Organization would miss this occasion for a farm, with a pig on it with four kinks in its tail. Now, naturally, any girl would long to walk up that Holy path with Nancy, but too many would spoil things; so, by drawing lots, Nancy had for company, Sarah Young, Lucy Donaldson, Priscilla Standish, Virginia Adams, Doris Johnson and Cora Grant; with Kathlyn as Maid of Honor, as charming an array of youthful glory as you could find in all Branton Hills.

Until this important arrival, Branton Hills' famous organist, just plain John Smith, was playing softly, "Just a Song at Twilight," watching for a signal from Mayor Gadsby; and soon swung into that famous march which brought forth a grand thrill, as tiny, blushing, palpitating Nancy took "Dad's" arm, gazing with shining orbs at that distant—oh, *so* distant—altar.

Now I want to know why anybody should want to *cry* on such a grand occasion. What is sad about it? But many a lash was moist as that tiny vision of glamorous purity slowly trod that fragrant pathway. Possibly girls can't avoid it; anyway, our Branton Hills girls didn't try to do so.

Gadsby, as has many a good old Dad, fought back any such showing; but I won't say that his thoughts didn't nag him; for, giving away your baby girl to any young, though first-class chap, is not actually *fun*. But that long, long trail finally brought him to that mossy dais, at which Frank, coming in through a handy door, stood waiting. Nancy was as calm as a wax doll; but Frank stood shaking with a most annoying cough (of imaginary origin!) as Pastor Brown stood, book in hand. Now I won't go through with all that was said; nor say anything about Nancy's tiny, warm, soft hand as it was put in Frank's big clumsy fist by Pastor Brown. Nor about that first Holy kiss; nor that long, mighty roar of organ music, as our happy, blushing pair trod that long pathway, door-wards. You know all about it, anyway, as most such rituals follow a standard custom. Nor shall I go into that happy hour at His Honor's mansion, during which that fancy loaf of frosting, raisins and citron was cut; (and which many a girl put in a pillow that night!); nor of that big bridal bunch of blossoms, which was thrown from a stairway into a happy group of hopping, jumping, laughing girls. (But I will say,— shhhh! that Kathlyn caught it!); nor anything of Nancy and Frank's thrilling trip to Branton Hills' big railway station, in that gift car which Nancy thought was a king's chariot; nor of a grand, low bow by old Pat Ryan of that station's trunk room. It was just that customary *"All aboard!!"* a crowd's "Hooray!—" and "Good Luck!!", with Branton Hills' Municipal Band a-blaring, and a mighty mob shouting and waving.

OH, HUM! I'll turn from this happy affair now and try to find out what was going on in this thriving, hustling city. Now you probably think of a city as a gigantic thing; for, if you go up onto a high hill, and look around across that vast array of buildings, parks, roads and distant suburbs, you not only think that it is a gigantic thing, you *know* it is. But, *is* it?

Just stop and think a bit. All such things as bulk, or width, you know by comparison only; comparison with familiar things. So, just for fun, go up in an imaginary balloon, about half way to that old Moon, which has hung aloft from your birth—(and possibly a day or two in addition)—and look down upon your "gigantic" city. How will it look? It is a small patch of various colors; but you know that, within that tiny patch, many thousands of your kind hurry back and forth; railway trains crawl out to far-away districts; and, if you can pick out a grain of dust that stands out dimly in a glow of sunlight, you may know that it is your mansion, your cabin or your hut, according to your financial status. Now, if that hardly shows up, how about *you?* What kind of a dot would *you* form in comparison? You must admit that your past thoughts as to your own pomposity will shrink just a bit! All this shows us that could this big World think, it wouldn't know that such a thing as Man was on it. And Man thinks that his part in all this unthinkably vast Cosmos is important! *Why,* you poor shrimp! if this old World wants to twitch just a bit and knock down a city or two, or split up a group of mountains, Man, with all his brain capacity, can only clash wildly about, dodging falling bricks. No. You wouldn't show up from that balloon as plainly as an ant, in crawling around our Capitol building at Washington.

But why all this talk about our own inconspicuosity? It is simply brought up to accompany Nancy's thoughts as that train shot across country; for Nancy, until now, had not known anything approaching such a trip. So this happy, happy trip, back upon which many a woman looks, with a romantic thrill, was astounding to such a girl. From Branton Hills to San Francisco; a boat to Honolulu, Manila, Shanghai, Hong Kong, Colombo, and finally Cairo. Ah! Cairo!! In thinking of it you naturally bring up two words—"Pyramids" and "Sphinx", words familiar from school days. Practically from birth, Nancy, along with millions of folks, had known that famous illustration of a thing half lion and half woman; and a mountainous mass of masonry, built for a king's tomb. So, standing right in front of both, Nancy and Frank got that wondrous thrill coming from attaining a long, long wish. From Cairo to Italy, Spain, London, Paris, and that grand Atlantic sail, landing at Boston, and hustling by fast train (but *how* slow it did go!!) to Branton Hills!

So, along about Thanksgiving Day, about half of its population was again at its big railway station, for Nancy was coming back. (And Frank, too, if anybody should ask you.)

And with that big Municipal Band a-booming and blaring, and a crowd of our old Organization girls pushing forward, did Branton Hills look good to Nancy? *And did Nancy look good to Branton Hills What* a glorious tan, from days and days on shipboard! And was that old Atlantic ugly? Ask Frank, poor chap, who, as on that big Pacific, had found out just what a ship's rail is for! And that stomachs can turn most amazing flip-flops if an old boat is too frisky!

In just an instant, actual count, Nancy was in Lady Gadsby's arms , fighting valiantly to hold back a flood of big, happy sobs; and Frank was busy, grabbing a cloud of hands surging towards him.

Coming back from a long trip is a happy occasion. And it is also mighty good to put a trunk or a bag down, knowing that it will "stay put" for a day or two, anyway. That constant packing and unpacking on a long trip, soon turns into an automatic function; and how Nancy did worry about what transportation customs in various lands would do to a first class trunk which has a romantic history, owing to its coming as a matrimonial gift from a group of loving girls. But now; ah! Put it away, and your things around, in familiar disposal.

Long trips do bring lots of fun and information; but a truly long trip is tiring, both in body and mind.

But Nancy and Frank won't stay with Gadsby long; for, during that trip, a charming bungalow was built on a lot of Gadsby's, facing City Park; and Nancy put in many days arranging things in it. Anybody who has had such joyful work to do, knows how assiduously a young pair would go about it; for two young robins carrying bits of cotton and string up to a criss-cross of twigs in a big oak, with *constant* soft, loving chirps, "had nothing," according to our popular slang, on Nancy and Frank.

Finally "moving in day" got around, with that customary party, to which you carry a gift to add to such things as a young husband on only a small salary can install. And *how* gifts did pour in!! Rugs, chairs, small stands, urns, clocks, photos in wall mountings, dainty scarfs (all hand-work by our girls in our Night School), books, lamps, a "radio" from Station KBH, until, finally, a big truck found an opportunity in that coming and going throng to back in and unload an upright piano, all satin ribbon wrappings, with a card "From Branton Hills' Municipal Band."

I COULD GO ON for hours about this starting out of Nancy and Frank, but many civic affairs await us; for Julius Gadsby, who has not got into this story up to now, had, from his constant poring through all kinds of books of information, built up a thorough insight into fossils; and you know that Kathlyn is *way* up in Biology; which brings in our awkward "bugs" again. Now bugs will burrow in soil, and always did, from History's birth; building catacombs which at last vanish through a piling up of rocks, sand or soil on that spot. Now Julius continually ran across accounts of important "finds" of such fossils, and with Kathlyn's aid was soon inaugurating popular clamor for a big Hall of Natural History.

This, Julius and Kathlyn thought, would turn out as popular, in a way, as living animals out at our Zoo. But an appropriation for a Hall of Natural History is a hard thing to jam through a City Council; for though its occupants call for no food, you can't maintain such a building without human custody; "which," said Old Bill Simpkins. "is but a tricky way of saying CASH!" But our Council was by now so familiar with calls from that famous "Organization", and, owing to its inborn faith in that grand body of hustling Youth, such a building was built; Julius and Kathlyn arranging all displays of fossil birds, plants, "bugs," footprints, raindrop marks, worms, skulls, parts of jaws, and so on. And what a crowd was on hand for that first public day! Julius and Kathlyn took visitors through various rooms, giving much data upon what was shown; and many a Branton Hills inhabitant found out a lot of facts about our vast past; about organisms living so far back in oblivion as to balk Man's brain to grasp. Kathlyn stood amongst groups of botanical fossilizations, with Gadsby not far away, as this studious young woman told school pupils how our common plants of today through various transitions in form, show a kinship with what now lay, in miraculously good condition, in this big Hall; and Julius told staring groups how this or that fossil did actually link such animals as our cow or walrus of to-day with original forms totally apart, both in looks and habits. And it was comforting to Gadsby to find pupils asking how long ago this was, and noting that amazing look as Julius had to say that nobody knows.

Such a building is an addition to any city; for this big World is so old that human calculation cannot fathom it; and it will, in all probability, go on always. So it is improving a child's mind to visit such displays; for it will start a train of thoughts along a path not commonly sought if such institutions do not stand as attractions. Now, in any community a crank will bob up, who will, with loud acclaim and high-sounding words, avow that it "is a scandalous drain on public funds to put up such a building just to show a lot of rocks, animals' ribs and birds' skulls." But such loud bombasts only show up an "orator's" brain capacity (or lack of it), and actually bring studious folks to ask for just such data upon things which his ridiculing had run down. It is an old, old story, that if you want a city's population to go in strongly for anything, and you start a loud, bawling campaign against it, that public will turn to it for information as to its worth. So, just such a loud, bawling moron had to drift into our Hall on its inauguration day, and soon ran smack up against Kathlyn! That worthy girl, allowing him to "blow off" a bit, finally said:—"I know you. You run a stock farm. All right. You want to know all you can about matching and crossing your stock, don't you? I thought so. But God did all that, long, oh, *so* long ago; gradually producing such animals as you own today; and all you can do is to follow along, in your puny way, and try to avoid a poor quality of stock mixing with yours. This building contains thousands of God's first works. It won't do you a bit of harm to look through our rooms. Nothing will jump out at you!"

At that that barking critic shut up! And Gadsby slid outdoors, chuckling:—"That's my girl talking!! That's my Kathlyn!!"

It is curious why anybody should pooh-pooh a study of fossils or various forms of rocks or lava. Such things grant us our only vision into Natural History's big book; and it isn't a book in first-class condition. Far from it! Just a tiny scrap; a slip; or, possibly a big chunk is found, with nothing notifying us as to how it *got* to that particular point, nor how long ago. Man can only look at it, lift it, rap it, cut into it, and squint at it through a magnifying glass. *And,—think* about it. That's all; until a formal study brings accompanying thoughts from many minds; and, by such tactics, judging that in all probability such and such a rock or fossil footprint is about so old. Natural History holds you in its grasp through just this impossibility of finding actual facts; for it is thus causing you to *think.* Now, thinking is not only a voluntary function; it is an *acquisition; an art.* Plants do not think. Animals probably do, but in a primary way, such as an aid in knowing poisonous foods, and how to bring up an offspring with similar ability. But Man can, and *should* think, and think hard and constantly. It is ridiculous to rush blindly into an action without looking forward to lay out a plan. Such an unthinking custom is almost a panic, and panic is but a mild form of insanity.

So Kathlyn and Julius did a grand, good thing in having this Hall as an addition to Branton Hills' institutions.

Now, in any city or town, or almost any small community, you will find a building, or possibly only a room, about which said city or town has nothing to say. It is that most important institution in which you put a stamp on your mail and drop it into a slot, knowing that it will find its way across city or country to that man or woman who is waiting for it.

But how many young folks know *how* this mail is put out so quickly. and with such guaranty against loss? Not many, I think, if you ask. So Gadsby, holding up Youth as a Nation's most important function in its coming history, thought that any act which would instruct a child in any way, was worthy. So, on a Saturday morning His Honor took a group of Grammar School pupils to a balcony in back of that all-hiding partition, and a postal official, showing all mail handling acts individually, said:—"In this country, two things stand first in rank: your flag and your mail. You all know what honor you pay to your flag, but you should know, also, that your mail—just that ordinary postal card—is also important. But a postal card, or any form of mail, is *not* important, in that way, until you drop it through a slot in this building, and with a stamp on it, or into a mail box outdoors. Up to that instant it is but a common card, which anybody can pick up and carry off without committing a criminal act. But as soon as it is in back of this partition, or in a mail box, a magical transformation occurs; and anybody who *now* should willfully purloin it, or obstruct its trip in any way, will find prison doors awaiting him. What a frail thing ordinary mail is! A baby could rip it apart, but no adult is so foolish as to do it. That small stamp which you stick on it, is, you might say, a postal official, going right along with it, having it always in his sight."

A giggling girl was curious to know if that was why a man's photo is on it. "Possibly," said our official, laughing. "But wait a bit. Look downstairs. As your mail falls in through that slot, or is brought in by a mailman, it is put through an ink-daubing apparatus—that's it, right down in front of you—which totally ruins its stamp. How about your man's photo, now?"

A good laugh rang around, and our official said:—"Now a man sorts it according to its inscription, puts it into a canvas bag and aboard a train, or possibly an aircraft. But that bag has mail going to points a long way apart, so a man in a mail car sorts it out, so that Chicago won't find mail in its bag which should go to California."

At this point our giggling girl said:—

"Ooooo! I had a Christmas card for Missouri go way down to Mississippi!"

How did you mark it?"

"I put M-i-s-s for Missouri."

"Try M-o, and I wish you luck."

As that laugh ran round, our official said:—"Now you know that you can buy a long, narrow stamp which will hurry your mail along. So, as all mail in this building is put up in many a small bunch, all with such stamps attract a mailman, who will so wrap a bunch that that kind of a stamp will show up plainly. Upon its arrival at a distant point, a boy will grab it, and hurry it to its final goal. But that stamp will not hurry it as long as it is on that train."

Our giggling girl, swinging in again, said:—"What? With that stamp right on top?"

"How can it?" said our official. "A train can only go just so fast, stamp or no stamp."

"Oh."

Our boys and girls got a big thrill from this visit in back of that partition, and told Gadsby so. On coming out of that building our party saw a big patrolman putting a small boy into a patrol wagon. That poor kid was but a bunch of rags, dirty, and in a fighting mood. Our boys got a big laugh out of it. Our girls, though, did *not*. Young Marian Hopkins who had that fairy wand, you know, at our airport inauguration, said:—

"Oh, that poor child! Will that cop put him in jail, Mayor Gadsby?" At which His Honor instantly thought of a plan long in his mind. Branton Hills had a court room, a child's court, in fact, at which a kindly man looks out for just such young waifs—trying to find out why such tots commit unlawful acts. So Gadsby said, "I don't know, Marian, but I want you young folks to go on a visit, tonight, to our night court, to find out about just such wild boys. How many want to go?"

To his satisfaction, all did; and so, that night that court room had rows of young folks, all agog with curiosity which a first visit to a court stirs up in a child. Just by luck, our young vagrant in rags was brought in first, shaking with childish doubt as to what was going to occur. But that kindly man sitting back of that big mahogany railing had no

54

thought of scaring a child, and said, calmly:—"Now, boy, what did you do that you ought not to do; and why did you do it?"

As our boys sat nudging and winking, but with our girls growing sad from sympathy, our young culprit said, *"Aw!* I grabs a bun, and dis big cop grabs my collar!"

"But why did you grab that bun? It wasn't yours, you know."

"Gosh, man!! I was *hungry!!"*

"Hungry? Don't your folks look out for you?"

"Naw; I do my own looking. And that's what I *was* doing, too!"

"What had you for food all day?"

"Just that bun. And *say!!* I only got *half* of it! That big cop was so rough!"

"Did that cop, as you call him, hurt you?"

"Hurt!! I should say *not!!* I put up a good stiff scrap! I paid him back, blow for blow! No big gas-bag of a cop is going to wallop *this* kid and not pay for it!"

"But, boy, don't your folks bring you up to know that it is wrong to rob anybody?"

"Naw! My Dad robs folks, and just got six months for it. So why shouldn't I? It's all right to do what your Dad will do, isn't it?"

"Not always, boy," and our girls in row two and our boys in row four sat sad and glum at this portrayal of youthful sin. Finally that big kindly man, thoughtfully rubbing his chin, said:—

"Whom did your Dad rob?"

"I dunno. It was a Ford car. Nobody wasn't in it, so why not grab it? That's what Dad said. You can pick up a bit of cash for a car, you know, boss. And say, if a car brung only six months, how long will I squat in jail for swiping this half bun? Aw! Go slow, boss! I ain't no bad kid! Only just a hungry mutt. Gosh!! *How* I wish I had a glass of milk!"

From row two a young, vigorous girlish form shot out, dashing for a doorway; and as that big kindly man was still rubbing his chin, Marian burst in again, rushing, sobbingly, to that sad bunch of rags, holding out a pint of milk and two hot biscuits. A quick snatch by two horribly dirty young hands, a limp flop on a mat at that big mahogany railing, and a truly hungry child was oblivious to all around him. And I'll say that our boys, in row four, had lumpy throats. But finally that big kindly man said:—"Though taking things unlawfully is wrong, conditions can occur in which so young a culprit is not at fault. This young chap has had no bringing up, but has run wild. A child will not know right from wrong if not taught; and, as it is a primary animal instinct to obtain food in any way, I will simply put this boy in a school which Branton Hills maintains for just such youths."

At this both row two and row four burst out in such a storm of hand-clapping that Gadsby found that this visit had shown his young folks, from actual contact with a child without training, how important child-raising is; and how proud a city is of such as act according to law.

IN ALMOST ANY big town, around Autumn, you will annually run across that famous agricultural show known as a County Fair; and, as Branton Hills had a big park, which you know all about, right in front of Nancy's and Frank's small bungalow, it was a most natural spot for holding it. And so, as this happy pair's third Autumn got around, stir-ring activity in that big park also got a-going; for railings for stockyards don't grow all built; yards and yards of brown canvas don't just blow into a park; nor do "hot dog" and popcorn stands jump up from noth-ing. And Nancy, rocking on that bungalow porch, could watch all this work going on. And rocking was about all that Nancy could, or, I should say, *should* do, just now.

What a sight it was! Trucks; small cars; wagons; a gang with a tractor plowing up hard spots; a gang picking up rocks, grading bumpy spots, and laying out ground plans. Masons building walls, and all kinds of goods arriving, by tons. But out of all that confusion and ado a canvas town will grow, strung from top to bottom with gaily flapping flags and hanging bunting, and that customary "mid-way" with its long rows of gaudy billboards, in front of which circus ballyhoo artists will continu-ously bawl and shout out claims about sword-swallowing, tattooing, hula-hula dancing, boa constrictor charming, or a Punch and Judy show.

At a County Fair two things stand out as most important: farm stock and that oval track around which swiftly trotting colts will thrill thou-sands; and, I'll say, shrink a bank account or two! But, of all sights, I don't know of any with such drawing ability for kids as just such a car-nival lot. So, daily, as soon as school was out, throngs of happy, shout-ing, hopping, jumping boys and girls would dash for that big park; looking, pointing, and climbing up on auto tops, into lofty oaks, onto tall rocks, or a pal's back; for if anything is difficult for a boy to obtain a sight of, nothing in climbing that an orang-outang can do, will balk him!

So Nancy sat calmly rocking, rocking, rocking, and,—but, pardon! I'll go on with this story. All I know is that Frank, arriving from work at Radio Station KBH, wouldn't so much as look at that big carnival lot, but would rush in, in a most loving, solicitous way which always brought a kiss and a blush from Nancy. Now if I don't quit talking about this young pair you won't know anything about that big show going up in front of that happy bungalow. Almost daily Lady Gadsby would drop in on Nancy, bringing all sorts of dainty foods; and His Honor, with Kathlyn, Julius and Bill, paid customary visits.

"But that fair!" you say. "How about that fair?"

Ah! It *was* a fair, I'll say! What mobs on that first day! And what a din!! Bands playing, ballyhoos shouting, popcorn a-popping, hot dogs a-sizzling, ducks squawking, cows lowing, pigs grunting, an occasional baby squalling; and 'midst it all, a choking cloud of dust, a hot Autumn wind, panting, fanning matrons, cussing husbands; all working toward that big oval track at which all had a flimsy possibility of winning a million or two (or a dollar or two!). Oh, you County Fairs! You bloom in your canvas glory, annually. You draw vast crowds; you show high quality farm stock, gigantic pumpkins, thousands of poultry, including our "Thanksgiving National Bird". You fill coops with fancy squabs, fat rabbits, and day-old chicks. You show many forms of incubators, churns, farming apparatus, pumps, plows, lighting plants for small farms, windmills, "bug" poisons, and poultry foods. And you always add a big balloon, which you anchor, so that kids may soar aloft until a windlass pulls it down. You fill us with food that would kill a wild goat, but you still last! And may you always do so; for, within your flapping, bulging canvas walls, city man rubs against town man, rich and poor girls bump, snobs attain no right of way, and a proud, happy boy or girl shows a "First Class" satin ribbon which a lovingly brought-up calf or poultry brood has won.

Only a satin ribbon, but, displaying it to a group of admiring young pals brings to a child that natural thrill from accomplishing anything worthy of public acclaim. Such thrills will not crowd in as Maturity supplants Youth; and so I say, "a trio of our customary huzzas" for any child who can carry away a satin ribbon from a County Fair.

But what about our good Mayor during all this circus hullabaloo? Did important thoughts for still improving Branton Hills pass through his busy mind? Not just now; but fond, anxious thoughts did; for his mind was constantly on Nancy; tiny, darling Nancy, his baby girl. For, during that noisy carnival, folks saw (or *thought* so, you know), a big bird with long shanks and a monstrous bill, circling round and round that small bungalow's roof, plainly looking for a spot to land on. Lady Gadsby and old Doctor Wilkins saw it, too, and told Nancy that that big hospital which our old Organization had built, was holding a room for instant occupancy; and, as that big bird daily swung down, down, down, almost grazing that small roof, Frank, poor chap, as shaky as at his church ritual, thirty months ago, staid away from Radio Station KBH, and stuck to that small bungalow as a fly sticks around a sugar bowl.

Finally, on a crisp Autumn night, that soaring bird shot straight down with such an assuring swoop, that old Doc Wilkins, indoors with Nancy, saw it and said, quickly:—

"On your way, Nancy girl!!" and that part of Branton Hills saw his car racing hospital-wards, with Lady Gadsby fondly patting Nancy's tiny, cold hands, and saying just such loving things as a woman would, naturally, to a young girl on such a trip. But Gadsby and Frank? Ah! Poor, half-crazy things! No car would do at all! *No, sir!!* A car was far too slow! And so, across lots, down into many a man's yard, and jumping high walls, shot two shadowy forms, arriving at that big hospital, badly blown, just as Lady Gadsby and old Doc Wilkins took Nancy's arms, and got slowly to that big door with its waiting rolling chair.

Now this stork's visit is nothing out of ordinary in World affairs. Millions and billions of visits has it, and its kind, flown—to king's mansion or a black Zulu woman's hut. But *this* flight was poor Frank's initiation to that awful hour of blank panic, during which a young husband is boiling hot or icy cold in turn. God!! How still a hospital corridor is!! How doctors and assistants do float past without as much sound as falling snow! Oh! *How* long Frank and His Honor sat, stood, or trod up and down, watching that room door!! What was going on? Was Nancy all right? Oh!! Why this prolonging of agonizing inactivity? Can't anybody say anything? *Isn't anybody around, at all?* But hospital doctors and nursing staffs, though pitying a young chap, must pass him up for that tiny lady, who now was but a tool in God's hands; in God's magic laboratory. And so Ah! Doctor Wilkins is coming—and smiling!!

"A baby girl—and with a ripping good pair of lungs!" but has to jump quick to catch Frank, who has sunk in a swoon. And Mayor Gadsby's collar is as limp as a dish-rag!

Ah! Man, man, man! and woman, woman, woman! Just you two! God's only parts in His mighty plan for living actuality. Not only with Man and animals, but also down—way, way down amongst plants. Just two parts. Only two!! And Baby, you tiny bunch of wriggling, gurgling humanity by that slowly ticking clock is your turn in this mighty World, unavoidably arriving. Mama, Papa, and all of us will go on, for a bit, growing old and gray, but you, now so young and frail. will stand sturdily, and willingly, in our vacancy; and carry on God's will!

AS THIS IS A history of a city I must not stay around any part too long. So, as it was almost "a small morning hour," Nina Adams, a widow, was sitting up; for Virginia, a High School girl, was still out; and, around two-thirty, was brought back in a fast car; two youths actually *dumping* an unconscious form on Nina's front porch, and dashing madly away. But Nina Adams saw it; and, calling for aid in carrying Virginia indoors, put in a frantic call for old Doc Wilkins, an old, long-ago school pal, who found Nina frantic from not knowing Virginia's condition, nor why that pair of youths shot madly away without calling anybody. But it only took Doctor Wilkins an instant to find out what was wrong; and Nina, noting his tight lips and growing scowl was in an agony of doubt.

"What *is* it, Tom? *Quick!!* I'm almost crazy!!"

Dr. Wilkins, standing by Virginia's couch, said, slowly:—

"It's nothing to worry about, Nina. Virginia will pull through all right, by morning."

But that didn't satisfy Nina Adams, *not for an instant,* and Dr. Wilkins, knowing that ironclad spirit of school days which would stand for no obstructions in its path, saw that a "blow-up" was coming; but, through a kindly thought for this woman's comfort, did not say what his diagnosis was, until Nina, now actually livid with worry, said:—

"Tom Wilkins! *Doctor* Wilkins, if you wish,—I claim a natural right to know why my child is unconscious! And you, a physician, cannot, by law, withhold such information."

But Wilkins, trying to find a way out of a most unhappy condition of affairs, said:—

"Now, Nina, you know I wouldn't hold anything from you if Virginia was critically ill, but that is not so. If you'll only wait until morning you'll find that I am right."

But this only built obstruction upon obstruction to Nina's strong will, until Dr. Wilkins, noticing coming total prostration, had to say:—

"Nina, Virginia is *drunk; horribly* drunk."

"Drunk!!" Widow Adams had to grab wildly at a chair, sinking into it; at first as limp as a rag, but instantly springing up, blood surging to a throbbing brow. *"Drunk! Drunk!! My* baby drunk!! Tom, I thank you for trying to ward off this shock; but I'll say right now, *with my hand on high,* that I am going to start a rumpus about this atrocity that will rock Branton Hills to its foundations! Who *got* this young school-girl drunk? I know that Virginia wouldn't drink that stuff willingly. How *could* it occur? I pay through taxation for a patrolman in this district; in fact in *all* districts of this city. What is a patrolman for, if not to watch for just such abominations as this, pray?"

Dr. Wilkins didn't say, though probably thinking of a rumor that had run around town for a month or two. At this point Virginia, partly conscious was murmuring:

"Oh, Norman! Oh! I'm *so* sick!!" *Don't!! I can't* drink it!

This brought forth all of Nina Adams' fury instantly.

Aha! Aha! Norman! So *that's* it! That's Norman Antor, that low-down, good-for-nothing night-owl! Son of our big Councilman Antor. So!! It's 'Norman! I can't drink it'!

Tom Wilkins, this thing is going to *court!!"*

~ ~ ~ ~ ~

ABOUT NOON OF that day, our good doctor, walking sadly along, ran across Mayor Gadsby, in front of City Hall; and did His Honor *"burn"* at such an abomination?

"What? High School boys *forcing* young girls to drink? And right in our glorious Branton Hills? Oh, but, Doc! This can't pass without a trial!"

"That's all right, John; but a thorn sticks out, right in plain sight."

"Thorn? Thorn? What kind of a thorn?" and our Mayor was flushing hard, as no kind of wild thoughts would point to any kind of thorns.

"That thorn," said Wilkins, "is young Norman Antor; son of–"

"Not of Councilman Antor?"

"I am sorry to say that it is so," and Wilkins told of Virginia's half-conscious murmurings. "And Nina wants to know why, with a patrolman in all parts of town, it isn't known that all this drinking is going on. I didn't say what I thought, but you know that a patrolman don't go into dancing pavilions and night clubs until conditions sanction it."

"Who is supplying this liquor?"

"Councilman Antor; but without knowing it.

All His Honor could say was to gasp:—

"How do you know that, Doc?" and Wilkins told of four calls for him in four days, to young *girls,* similarly drunk.

"And my *first* call was to young Mary—Antor's tiny Grammar School kid, who was as drunk as Virginia; but, on coming out of it, told of robbing Antor's pantry, in which liquor was always on hand for his political pals, you know; that poor kid taking it to various affairs and giving it to boys; and winning 'popularity' that way."

"So," said Gadsby, "Councilman Antor's boy and girl, brought up in a family with liquor always handy. now, with ignorant, childish braggadocio, bring Councilman Antor into this mix—up! I'm sorry for Antor; but his pantry is in for an official visit.

It wasn't so long from this day that Court got around to this rumpus. To say that that big room was *full,* would put it mildly. Although, according to an old saying, "a cat is only as big as its skin," that room's walls almost burst, as groups of church organizations and law abiding inhabitants almost fought for admission; until standing room was nothing but a suffocating jam. As Gadsby and Doc Wilkins sat watching that sight, Gadsby said:—"It's an outpouring of rightful wrath by a proud city's population; who, having put out good, hard work in bringing it to its high standing as a community, today, will not stand for anything that will put a blot on its municipal flag, which is, right now, proudly flying on City Hall."

As Wilkins was about to say so, a rising murmur was rolling in from out back, for Norman Antor was coming in, in custody of a big patrolman, and with four youths, all looking, not only anxious, but plainly showing humiliation at such an abomination against trusting young girlhood. Scowls and angry rumblings told that high official, way up in back of that mahogany railing, that but a spark would start a riot. So, in a calm, almost uncanny way, this first trial of its kind in Branton Hills got along to a court official calling, loudly:—"Virginia Adams!

If you think that you know what a totally still room is, by no kink of your imagination could you possibly know such an awful, frightful *hush* as struck that crowd dumb, as Virginia, a tall, dark, willowy, stylish girl quickly took that chair, from which Truth, in all its purity, is customarily brought out, But Virginia was not a bit shaky nor anxious, nor doubtful of an ability to go through with this ugly task.

Gadsby and Doc Wilkins sat watching Nina; Gadsby with profound sympathy, but Wilkins with an old school-pal's intuition, watching for a blowup. But Nina didn't blow up, that is, not visibly: but that famous rigid will was boiling, full tilt; boiling up to a point for landing, "tooth and claw" on our pompous Councilman's son, if things didn't turn out satisfactorily.

Virginia didn't occupy that stand long; it was only a half-sobbing account of a night at a dancing pavilion; and with a sob or two from a woman or girl in that vast crowd. All Virginia said was:—"Norman Antor said I was a cry-baby if I wouldn't drink with him. But I said, 'All right; I *am* a cry-baby! And I always *will* turn 'crybaby' if anybody insists that I drink that stuff." (Just a short lull, a valiant fight for control, and)—

"But I *had* to drink!! Norman was tipping my chair back and John Allison was forcing that glass into my mouth! I got so sick I couldn't stand up, and didn't know a thing until I found I was on a couch in my own parlor."

A court official said, kindly:—

"That will do, Miss Adams."

During this, Nina was glaring at Norman; but Virginia's bringing Allison into it, also, was too much. But Wilkins, watching narrowly, said, snappingly:—

"Nina! This is a *court room."*

Now this trial was too long to go into, word for word; so I'll say that not only Norman Antor and Allison, but also our big, pompous Councilman Antor, according to our popular slang, "got in bad"; and Branton Hills' dancing and night spots got word to prohibit liquor or shut up shop. Young Mary Antor was shown that liquor, in dancing pavilions or in a family pantry was not good for young girls; and soon this most disgusting affair was a part of Branton Hills' history. And what vast variations a city's history contains! What valorous acts by far-thinking officials! What dark daubs of filth by avaricious crooks! What an array of past Mayors; what financial ups and downs; what growth in population. But, as I am this particular city's historian, *with strict orthography controlling it,* this history will not rank, in volubility, with any by an author who can sow, broadcast, all handy, common words which *continuously* try to jump into it!

BRANTON HILLS, now an up-to-today city, coming to that point of motorizing all city apparatus, had just a last, solitary company of that class which an inhabitant frantically calls to a burning building— Company Four, in our big shopping district; all apparatus of which was still animal drawn; four big, husky chaps: two blacks and two roans. Any thought of backing in any sort of motor apparatus onto this floor, upon which this loyal four had, during many' months, stood, champing at bits, pawing and whinnying to start out that big door, in daylight or night-gloom, calm or storm,—was mighty tough for old Dowd and Clancy. A *man* living day and night with such glorious, vivacious animals, grows to look upon such as almost human. Bright, brainy, sparkling colts can win a strong hold on a man, you know.

And now!! What form of disposal was awaiting "Big Four", as Clancy and Dowd took a fond joy in dubbing this pair of blacks and two roans? Clancy and Dowd didn't know anything but that a mass of cogs, piping, brass railings, an intricacy of knobs, buttons, spark-plugs, forward clutch and so forth was coming tomorrow.

"Aw!!' said Dowd, moaningly, "you know, Clancy, that good old light shifting about and that light 'stomping' in that row of stalls, at night; you know, old man, that happy crunching of corn; that occasional cough; that tail-swatting at a fly or crazy zigzagging moth; that grand animal odor from that back part of this floor."

"I do," said Clancy. "And *now* what? A loud whizz of a motor! A suffocating blast of gas! and a dorn thing a-standin' on this floor, wid no brain; wid nothin' lovin' about it. Wid no soul."

"Um-m-m," said Dowd, "I dunno about an animal havin' a soul, but it's got a thing not so dom far *from* it."

As Clancy sat worrying about various forms of disposal for Big Four, an official phoning from City Hall, said just an ordinary, common word, which had Clancy bopping up and down, *furiously mad.*

"What's all this? What's all this?" Dowd sang out, coming from a stall, in which a good rubbing down of a shiny coat, and continuous loving pats had brought snuggling and nosing.

"Auction!!" said Clancy, wildly, and sitting down with a thud.

"Auction? Auction for Big Four? What?

Put up on a block as you would a Jap urn or a phony diamond?"

"Uh-huh; that's what City Hall says.

An awful calm slunk insidiously onto that big smooth floor, as Dowd and Clancy, chins on hands, sat,—just thinking! Finally Clancy burst out with:—

"Aw! If an alarm would *only* ring in, right now, to stop my brain from cracking! *Auction! Bah!!"*

~ ~ ~ ~ ~

A BIG CROWD STOOD in City Park, including His Honor, many a Councilman, and, naturally, Old Bill Simpkins, who was always bound to know what was going on. A loud, fast-talking man, on a high stand, was shouting:—"All right, you guys! How much? How much for this big black? A mountain of muscular ability! Young, kind, willing, smart! How much? How much?"

Bids abominably low at first, but slowly crawling up; crawling slowly, as a boa constrictor crawls up on its victim. But, *without fail,* as a bid was sung out from that surging, gawking, chin-lifting mob, a woman, way in back, would surpass it! And that woman hung on, as no boa constrictor could! Gadsby, way down in front, couldn't fathom it, at all. Why should a woman want Big Four? A solitary animal, possibly, but *four!* So His Honor, turning and making his way toward that back row, ran smack into Nancy.

"Daddy! Lady Standish is outbidding all this crowd I"

"Oho! So *that's* it!"

So Gadsby, pushing his way again through that jam, and coming to that most worthy woman, said:—

"By golly, Sally! It's plain that you want Big Four."

"John Gadsby, you ought to *know* that I do. Why! A man might buy that big pair of roans to hitch up to a plow! Or hook a big black onto an ash cart!"

"I know that, Sally, but that small back yard of yours is—"

"John!! Do your Municipal occupations knock all past days' doings out of your skull? You *know* that I own a grand, big patch of land out in our suburbs, half as big as Branton Hills. So this Big Four will just run around, jump, roll, kick, and loaf until doomsday, if I can *wallop* this mob out of bidding."

As Lady Standish was long known as standing first in valuation on Branton Hills' tax list, nobody in that crowd was so foolish as to hang on, in a war of bidding, against *that* bankroll. So Gadsby shook hands, put an arm about Nancy, walking happily away, as a roar of plaudits shot out from that crowd, for that loud, fast-talking man was announcing:—*"Sold! All four to Lady Standish!!"*

As Gadsby and Nancy ran across Old Bill Simpkins, Gadsby said:—
"Bill, *you* know that grand old day.

Look! A building is burning! A patrolman has put in an alarm! And *now* look! Corning down Broadway! Two big blacks, and following on, two big roans! What grand, mighty animals! Nostrils dilating; big hoofs pounding; gigantic flanks bulging; mighty lungs snorting; monstrous backs straining; thick, full tails standing straight out. Coming, sir! Coming, sir!! Just as fast as brain and brawn can! And that gong-clanging, air-splitting, whistling, shining, sizzling, smoking four tons of apparatus roars past, grinding and hanging on Broadway's paving! *You* saw all that, Bill."

"Uh-huh," said Simpkins, "but a motor don't hurt our paving so much."

As Nancy took His Honor's arm again, Gadsby said:—"Poor, cranky old Bill! Always running things down."

But how about Clancy and Dowd? On moving out from that big park, that happy pair, if Knighthood was in bloom today, would bow low, and kiss fair Lady Standish's hand.

OH HUM. Now that Nancy's baby is gurgling or squalling, according to a full tummy, or tooth conditions; and Nancy is looking, as Gadsby says, "as good as a million dollars," I find that that busy young son-of-a-gun, Dan Cupid, is still snooping around Branton Hills And now who do you think is hit? Try to think of a lot of girls in Gadsby's old Organization Youth. No, it's not Sarah Young, nor Lucy Donaldson, nor Virginia Adams. It was brought to your historian in this way:—

Lady Gadsby and His Honor sat around his parlor lamp, His Honor noticing that Lady G. was smiling, finally saying:—
"John."
"Uh-huh."
"Kathlyn and John Smith—"
"What?"

"I said that Kathlyn and John Smith want to—"

"Oho! Aha!! I'll call up Pastor Brown to start right off dolling up his big church!"

"No, no! Not now! Wait about six months. This is only a troth. Folks don't jump into matrimony, that way.

"Hm-m-m! I don't know about that," said Gadsby, laughing; and thinking way back to that captivating lassoo!

John Smith was Branton Hills' famous church organist; and, at a small, dainty lunch, Kathlyn told of this troth. In a day or two about all Branton Hills' young girlhood had, on rushing in, told Kathlyn what a grand chap John was; and all that town's young manhood had told John similar things about Kathlyn. So, as this is a jumpy sort of a story, anyway, why not skip months of happy ardor, and find how this tying of an additional knot in our Mayor's family will turn out? You know that Kathlyn don't think much of pomp or show, and such a big church ritual as Nancy had is all right if you want it, but Kathlyn had fond thoughts of just a small, parlor affair, with only a group of old chums; and no throwing of old boots, and "sharp food-grains," which work downward, to scratch your back, or stick in your hair as stubbornly as burrs.

"Such crazy doings," said Kathlyn, "always look foolish. It's odd how anybody can follow up such antiquarian customs."

As Kathlyn's big night was drawing nigh, Lady Gadsby and Nancy had constantly thought of a word synonymous with "woman", and that word is "scrub." Which is saying that Gadsby's mansion was about to submit to a gigantic scrubbing, painting, dusting, and so forth, so that Kathlyn should start out on that ship of matrimony from a spic-span wharf. Just why a woman thinks that a grain of dust in a totally incon-spicuous spot is such a catastrophic abnormality is hard to say; but if you simply broach a thought that a grain of it might lurk in back of a piano, or up back of an oil painting, a flood of soap-suds will instantly burst forth; and any man who can find any of his things for four days is a clairvoyant, or a magician!

As Gadsby sat watching all this his thoughts took this form:—

"Isn't it surprising what an array of things a woman can drag forth, burrowing into attics, rooms and nooks! Things long out of mind; an old thing; a worn-out thing; but it has lain in that room, nook or bag until just such a riot of soap and scrubbing brush brings it out. And, as I think of it, a human mind could, and should go through just such a ransacking, occasionally; for you don't know half of what an accumulation of rubbish is kicking about, in its dark, musty corridors. Old fashions in thoughts; bigotry; vanity; all lying stagnant. So why not drag out and sort all that stuff, discarding all which is of no valuation? About half of us will find, in our minds, a room, having on its door a card, saying: "It Was Not So In My Day." Go at that room, right off. That "My Day" is long past. "Today" is boss, now. If that "My Day" could crawl up on "Today," what a mix-up in World affairs would occur! Ox cart against aircraft; oil lamps against arc lights! Slow, mail information against radio! But, as all this stuff is laid out, what will you do with it? Nobody wants it. So I say, burn it, and tomorrow morning, how happy you will find that musty old mind!"

But His Honor's mansion finally got back to normal as clouds of dust and swats and slaps from dusting cloths had shown Lady Gadsby and Kathlyn that "that parlor was simply awful" though Gadsby, Julius and Bill always had thought that "It looks all right," causing Kathlyn to say:—

"A man thinks all dust stays outdoors."

Though marrying off a girl in church is a big proposition, it can't discount, in important data, doing a similar act in a parlor; for, as a parlor is a mighty small room in comparison with a church, you can't point to an inch of it that won't do its small part on such an occasion; so a woman will find about a thousand spots in which to put tacks from which to run strings holding floral chains, sprays, or small lights. So Gadsby, Bill and Julius, with armfuls of string and mouthfuls of tacks, not only put in hours at pounding said tacks, but an occasional vigorous word told that a thumb was substituting! But what man wouldn't gladly bang his thumb, or bark his shins on a wobbly stool, to aid so charming a girl as Kathlyn? And, on that most romantically important of all days!!

Anyway, that day's night finally cast its soft shadows on Branton Hills. Night, with its twinkling stars, its lightning-bugs, and its call for girls' most glorious wraps; and youths' "swallowtails", and tall silk hats,—is Cupid's own; lacking but organ music to turn it into Utopia.

And was Gadsby's mansion lit up from porch to roof? No. Only that parlor and a room or two upstairs, for wraps, mascara, a final hair-quirk, a dab of lip-stick; for Kathlyn, against all forms of "vain display," said:—"I'm only going to marry a man; not put on a circus for all Branton Hills."

"All right, darling," said Gadsby, "you shall marry in a pitch dark room if you wish; for, as you say, a small, parlor affair is just as binding as a big church display. It's only your vows that count."

So but a small group stood lovingly in Gadsby's parlor, as Parson Brown brought into unity Kathlyn and John. Kathlyn was radiantly happy; and John, our famous organist, was as happy with only charming Sarah Young at an upright piano, as any organist in a big choir loft.

But to Lady Gadsby and His Honor, this was, in a way, a sad affair; for that big mansion now had lost two of its inhabitants; and, as many old folks know, a vast gap, or chasm thus forms, backward across which flit happy visions of laughing, romping, happy girlhood; 'happy hours around a sitting room lamp; and loving trips in night's small hours to a room or two, just to know that a small girl was all right, or that a big girl was not in a draft. But, though marrying off a girl will bring such a vacancy, that happy start out into a world throbbing with vitality and joy, can allay a bit of that void in a big mansion, or a small cabin. A birth, a tooth, a growth, a mating; and, again a birth, a tooth, and so on. Such is that mighty Law, which was laid down on that first of all days; and which will control Man, animal, and plant until that last of all nights.

So it was first Nancy, and now Kathlyn; and Branton Hills' gossips thought of Bill and Julius, with whom many a young, romantic maid would gladly sit in a wistaria-drooping arbor on a warm, moon-lit night; flighty maids with Bill, adoring his high class social gossip; studious maids with Julius, finding much to think about in his practical talks on physics, zoology, and natural history. Tho Bill and Julius had shown no liability of biting at any alluring bait on any matrimonial hook; and Gadsby, winking knowingly, would say:—

"Bill is too frivolous, just now; and Julius too busy at our Hall of Natural History. But just wait until Dan Cupid starts shooting again, and watch things whiz!"

SARAH, WALKING along past City Park on a raw, cold night, found a tiny,—oh *so* tiny,—puppy, whining, shaking and crying *with* cold, Picking up that small bunch of babyhood, Sarah was in quandary as just what to do; but Priscilla Standish, coming along, said:—"Oh! Poor baby!! Who owns him, Sarah?"

"I don't know; but say! Wouldn't your Ma—?"

"My Ma *would!!* Bring him along, and wrap your cloak around him. It's awfully cold for so young a puppy.

So Lady Standish, with that "back-yard *zoo* soon bad his quaking babyship lapping good warm milk, and a stumpy tail wagging as only a tiny puppy's stumpy tail *can wag*. Along towards six o clock a vigorous pounding on Lady Standish's front door brought Priscilla, to find Old Bill Simpkins with a tiny, wildly sobbing girl of about four. Walking into Lady Standish's parlor, Simpkins said:

"This kid has lost a-a-a-crittur; I think it was a pup, wasn't it, kid?"

A vigorous up and down bobbing of a small shock of auburn hair.

"So," said Simpkins, "I thought it might show up in your back-yard gang."

"It has, Bill, you *old grouch!!*' for Lady Standish, as about all of Branton Hills grown-ups, was in school with Bill. "It's all right, now, and warm and cuddly. Don't cry, Mary darling. Priscilla will bring in your puppy.

As that happy baby sat crooning to that puppy, also a baby, Old Bill had to snort out:—"Huh! A lot of fuss about a pup, I'll say!"

"Oh, *pooh-pooh,* Bill Simpkins!" said Lady S.

"Why *shouldn't* a child croon to a puppy? Folks bring all kinds of animals to my back yard, if sick or hurt. Want to walk around my *zoo?*"

"*No!!* No zoos for Councilman Simpkins! Animals ain't worth so much fuss!"

"Pshaw, Bill! You talk ridiculously! I wish you could know of about half of my works. I want to show you a big Angora cat. A dog bit its foot so I put a balm on it and wound it with cotton—"

"You put *balm* on a *cat's* foot!! *Bah!*"

But Lady Standish didn't mind Old Bill's ravings having known him so long; so said:—

"Oh, how's that old corn of yours? Can't I put a balm—"

"*No!* You cannot! Mary, bring your pup; I'm going along."

As a happy tot was passing out that big, kindly front door, Sarah said "Was Councilman Simpkins always so grouchy, Lady Standish?"

"No. Not until John Gadsby 'cut him out' and won Lady Gadsby."

"Aha!! And a Ho, Ho!!" said Sarah, laughing gayly. "So folks had what you call 'affairs' way back, just as today!" and also laughing inwardly, at what Lucy had said about this kindly Lady Standish and His Honor.

Ah! That good old schoolday, now so long past! How it bobs up, now-a-days, if you watch a young lad and a happy, giggling lass holding hands or laughing uproariously at youthful witticisms. And how diaphanous and almost imaginary that far-back day looks, if that girl with whom you stood up and said "I do," laughs, if you try a bit of romantic kissing, and says:—

"Why, John! How silly! You act actually childish!!"

~ ~ ~ ~ ~

AND NOW IT WON'T do any harm to hark back a bit on this history, to find how our big Night School is doing. Following that first graduation day, many and many a child, and adult, too, had put in hours on various nights; and if you visit it you will find almost as many forms of instruction going on as you will find pupils; for thousands of folks today know of topics which, with a bit of study, could turn out profitably. Now Branton Hills had, as you know, built this school for public instruction; and, as with all such institutions, visiting days occur. And *what* a display of goods and workmanship! And what bright, happy pupils, standing proudly back of it! For mankind knows hardly a joy which will surpass that of approval of his work.

Gadsby's party first took in a wood-working shop; finding small stands which fit so happily into many a living room nook; book racks for walls or floor; moth-proof bins, smoking stands, many with fancy uprights or inlaid tops; high chairs for tiny tots; arm chairs for old folks; cribs, tobacco humidors, stools, porch and lawn swings, ballbats, rolling pins, mixing boards; in fact about anything that a man can fashion from wood.

As an indication of practical utility coming from such public instruction, a man told Gadsby:—

"I didn't know much about wood-working tools until I got into this class. This thing I am making would cost about thirty dollars to buy, but all it cost, so far, is two dollars and a half, for wood and glass," which Gadsby thought was worth knowing about; as so many of his Council had put forth so many complaints against starting such a school without charging for instruction. In an adjoining room His Honor's party found boys banging and pounding happily; and, if you should ask,—noisily,—on brasswork: making bowls, trays, lamp standards, photograph stands, book supports and similar artistic things.

Across from that was a blacksmith shop, with its customary flying sparks and sizzling cooling-vats.

But, by going upstairs, away from all this din, Gadsby, humming happily, found Sarah and Lucy, Nancy and Kathlyn amidst a roomful of girls doing dainty fancy-work. And what astonishing ability most of that group *did* show! Nancy bought a baby-cap which was on a par with anything in Branton Hills' shops; and though Kathlyn said it was "just too cunning for anything", John Smith's bungalow didn't contain any- body (just now!) whom it would fit.

But Lady Gadsby, with a party of Branton Hills matrons, was calling for Gadsby to hurry down a long corridor to a loom-room, saying that such dainty rugs, mats and scarfs of cotton and silk hung all around on walls or racks, it was truly astonishing that girls could do such first- class *work*, having had long hours of labor in Broadway's shops all day.

Although most of our standard occupations found room for activity, an occasional oddity was run across. So His Honor's party found two boys and two girls working at that always fascinating art of glass- blowing. And what a dainty trick it is! And what an opportunity to burn a thumb or two, if you don't wait for things to cool! Things of charm- ing form *and* fragility, grow as by a magician's wand, from small glass tubings of various colors. Birds with glorious wings, ships of crystal sailing on dark billows, tiny buildings in a thick glass ball which upon agitation, stirs up a snowstorm which softly lands on pink roof-tops; many a fancy drinking glass and bowl, oil lamps, ash trays, and gaudy strings of tiny crystal balls for adorning party gowns. And did Nancy want to buy out this shop? And did Frank doubt his ability to do so? And did Kathlyn ask: "How about it, Johnny?" and did John Smith say: "Nothing doing"? It was just that. But it only shows that good old Branton Hills' inclination for aiding anything which looks worthy; and such a school I know you will admit, looks that way.

Tramping upstairs, still again, Gadsby and party found a class so varying from all downstairs as to bring forth murmurs of joy, for this was known as "Music Floor"; upon which was taught all forms of that most charming of all arts—from solo work to community singing, from solitary violin pupil to a full brass band. On our party's arrival, Lucy, Doris and Virginia, hurrying from classrooms, sang, in trio, that soft, slow Italian song, "O Solo Mio;" and, as Gadsby proudly said, "Not for many a day had such *music* rung out in Branton Hills*;"* for most girls, if in training with a practical vocalist, *can* sing; and most charmingly.

In a far room was a big string outfit of banjos, mandolins and guitars, happily strumming out a smart, throbbing Spanish fandango, until His Honor could not avoid a swinging of body and tapping of foot; causing Lady Gadsby to laugh, saying:—

"Rhythm has a mighty grip on Zulus, I am told."

To which our swaying Mayor said:—

"Anyway, a Zulu has a lot of fun out of it. If singing, playing and dancing could only crowd out sitting around and moping, folks would find that a Zulu can hand us a tip or two on happy liv*ing."*

But all music is not of string form; so, in a big auditorium, our party found a full brass band of about fifty boys, with a man from Branton Hills' Municipal Band as instructor. Now as Gadsby was, as you boys say, "not at all bad" on a big bass horn in his youthful days, this band instructor, thinking of it, was asking him to "sit it" and play. So, as Lady Gadsby, two girls, and two sons-in-law sat smiling and giggling in a front row, and as fifty boys could hardly play, from laughing, that big horn got such a blasting that it was practically a horn solo! And Nancy, doubling up from giggling, said:—"D-d-daddy! If-f-f-f B-b-b-barnum's circus hits town, you must join its cl-cl-clown band!"

But I had to rush this happy party out of that building, as an awful thing was occurring but a block from it; which told its own story by a lurid light, flashing through windows; clanging gongs, shrilling horns and running, shouting crowds; for an old, long-vacant factory building just across from City Hall, was blazing furiously. Rushing along Broadway was that "motor thing," with Clancy and Dowd clinging wildly on a running board. Pulling up at a hydrant, Clancy said to His Honor:—

"As I was a-hangin' onto this dom thing, a-thinkin' it was going to bang into a big jam at two crossroads, I says, 'By Gorra! that big pair of blacks wouldn't bang into *nuthin'!* But this currazy contraption! It ain't got no brain—no nuthin, no soul—nuthin' but halitosis!!"

As Gadsby took a long look at Clancy's "dom thing, a vision was wafting through his mind of a calm, sunny patch of land, way out in Branton Hills' suburbs, on which day by day, two big blacks and two big roans could—anyway, taking all things into account, a big conflagration, with its din, rush and panic, is no spot for such animals as Big Four." As for Old Bill's squawk about animals "ruining our paving,"

Gadsby thought that was but small talk, for paving, anyway, can't last for long. But, that *is* a glorious spot, way out amongst our hills!

Gadsby took his party to a room in City Hall from which that burning factory was in plain sight; and as Nancy and Kathlyn stood watching that awful sight a big wall, crashing down, had a crowd rushing to that spot.

A man's form was brought out to a patrol wagon; and a boy, rushing past City Hall, sang out to Gadsby "It's Old Man Donaldson! Tiny Nancy, almost swooning, said:—

"Donaldson? Oh, Kathy! That's Lucy's Dad, of Company Two, you know!" and Frank and John Smith shot wildly downstairs to find out about it. In an instant a sobbing girlish form was dashing madly from that Night School building towards our Municipal Hospital. It was Lucy; bright, always laughing Lucy; but half an hour ago singing so happily in that girls' trio.

As that big factory was still blazing furiously, Frank and John, coming in, said:—

"It was only a scalp wound, and a sprung wrist. Lucy is coming upstairs, now." Lucy, coming in, badly blown from running and fright, said:—

"That wall caught Daddy; but it was so old and thin it didn't crush him. Oh! *How* I worry if that alarm rings!"

"But," put in Nancy, "it's *man's* work. Pshaw!! What good am *I?* Why, I couldn't do a thing around that factory, right now! Look at my arm! About as big as a ball bat*!* " and as Frank took that sad, tiny form in his arms, Gadsby said:—

"All throughout Natural History, Nancy, you will find man built big and strong, and woman small and frail. That is so that man can obtain food for his family, and that woman may nourish his offspring. But today, I am sorry to say, you'll find girls working hard, in gymnasiums, fondly hoping to attain man's muscular parity. How silly!! It's going straight against all natural laws. Girls *can* find a lot of bodily good in gymnasiums, I'll admit! but *not* that much. And as for your 'ball-bat' arm, as you call it, what of it? You'd look grand, now wouldn't you, with Frank's big oak-branch arms hanging way down to your shins. But that ball-bat arm can curl around your tiny baby as softy as a down pillow. Aw, darling! *Don't* say you can't do anything; for *I* know you can. How about our old Organization of Youth days? You,—"

And Nancy, now laughing, said, gaily:—

"Oho! Our old Organization! What fun it was! But, Daddy, I don't know of any young crowd following us up.

"No. Our young folks of today think such things too much work;" and, as that old factory was but a mass of ruins now, and midnight was approaching, Gadsby's family was soon in that mythical Land of Nod, in which no horns blow, no sparks fall; only occasionally a soft gurgling from a crib in Nancy's bungalow.

IT IS AN ODD kink of humanity which cannot find any valuation in spots of natural glory. But such kinks do run *riot* in Man's mind, occasionally, and Branton Hills ran up against such, on a Council night; for a bill was brought up by Old Bill Simpkins for disposal of City Park to a land company, for building lots! At first word of such a thought, Gadsby was totally dumb, from an actual impossibility of thinking that *any* man, bringing tip such a bill, wasn't plumb crazy!

"What! Our main Park; including our Zoo?"

"Just that," said Simpkins. "Just a big patch of land, and a foolish batch of animals that do nobody any good. You can't hitch a lion up to a city-dump cart, you know; nor a hippopotamus to a patrol wagon. What good *is* that bunch of hair and horns, anyway? And that park! *Wait!!* Just grass, grass, grass! Branton Hills pay's for planting that grass, pays for sprinkling it, pays for cutting it—arid *throws it* away! So I say, put it into building lots, and draw good, solid cash from it."

An Italian Councilman, Tony Bandamita was actually boiling during this outburst; and, in a flash, as Simpkins quit, was up, shouting:—

"I gotta four bambinos. My bambinos playa in thatta park: run, jumpa and rolla. Grow bigga an strong. My woman say no coulda do thatta if playa all day on bricka walks. I say no buncha land sharks buya thatta Park!! How many you guys go to it, anyway? Huh? Notta many! But *go!!* Walk around; sniffa its blossoms; look at grand busha; sit on softa grass! You do thatta, an' *I* know you not stick no building on it!!"

So, at Mayor Gadsby's instigation, Council did not ballot on Simpkins' bill; and said it would go, as Tony thought only right, and "look atta gooda busha."

In a day or two this pompous body of solons was strolling about that big park. No man with half a mind could fail to thrill at its vistas of shrubs, ponds, lawns, arbors, fancy fowl, small pavilions and curving shady pathways. As Gadsby was "takinga his owna looka," Old Bill Simpkins, coming a-snorting and a-fussing along, sang out, gruffly:—

"All right; this is it! This is that grand patch of grass that pays Branton Hills no tax!"

But Gadsby was thinking—and thinking hard, too. Finally saying:—

"Bill, supposing that any day you should walk along that big Pathway known in Sunday School as 'Our Straight But Narrow Way.' You would find coming towards you, all sorts of folks: a king, roaring past in his big chariot, a capitalist with his bands full of bonds, an old, old lady, on a crutch. Such passings would bring to you various thoughts. But, supposing it was a possibility that you saw *Bill Simpkins* coming your way. Aha! What an opportunity to watch that grouchy old—"

"That *what?*"

"I'll say it again: that grouchy old crab. How you *would* gawk at him, that most important of all folks, to you. How you would look at his clothing, his hat, his boots! That individual would pass an inquiry such as you had not thought it a possibility to put a man up against. Bill, I think that if you *should* pass Councilman Simpkins on that Big Pathway, you would say: 'What a grouchy old crittur that was!"

Old Bill stood calmly during this oration, and, looking around that big park, said:—

"John, you know how to talk, all right, all right. I'll admit that things you say do do a lot of good around this town. But if I should run across this guy you talk about, on that vaporous highway, or 'boardwalk', as *I* should call it,—I'd say, right out good and loud: "Hi! You!! Hurry back to Branton Hills and put up a block of buildings in that silly park!" and Gadsby, walking away, saw that an inborn grouch is as hard to dig out as a wisdom tooth.

Now this Council's visit on this particular day, was a sly plan of Gadsby's, for His Honor is, you know, Youth's Champion, and having known many an occasion on which Youth has won out against Council opposition. So, our big City officials, strolling around that park, soon saw a smooth lawn upon which sat, stood, or ran, almost a thousand small tots of from four to six. In dainty, flimsy outfits, many carrying fairy wands, it was a sight so charming as to thaw out a brass idol! Amidst this happy party stood a tall shaft, or mast, having hanging from its top a thick bunch of long ribbons, of pink, lilac, gray, and similar dainty colors; and around it stood thirty tots—thirty tiny fists all agog to grasp thirty gay ribbons. Old Bill took a look, and said, growlingly, to His Honor:—

"What's all this stuff, anyway?"

"Bill, and Branton Hills' Council," said Gadsby, "today is May Day—that day so symbolic of budding blossoms, mating birds and sunny sky. You all know, or *ought* to, of that charming custom of childhood of toddling round and round a tall mast, in and out, in and out,—thus winding gay ribbons about it in a spiral. That is but a small part of what this Park can do for Branton Hills. But it is an important part; for happy childhood grows up into happy adults, and happy adults"—looking right at Councilman Simpkins—*"can* form a happy City Council."

Now a kid is always a kid; and a kid knows just how any sport should go. So, just by luck, a tot who was to hold a gay ribbon didn't show up; and that big ring stood waiting, for that round-and-round march just *couldn't* start with a ribbon hanging down! But a kid's mind is mighty quick and sharp; and a small tot of four had that kind of mind, saying:—

"Oh! That last ribbon! Isn't anybody going to hold it?"

Now historians shouldn't laugh. Historians should only put down what occurs. But I, *your* historian of Branton Hills, not only had to laugh, but to *roar;* for this tot, worrying about that hanging ribbon, saw our big pompous Council group looking on. Now a Council is nothing to a tot of four; just a man or two, standing around. So, trotting up and grasping Old Bill's hand, this tot said:

"You'll hold it, won't you?"

"What!!" and Simpkins was all colors on throat and brow as Branton Hills' Council stood, grinning. But that baby chin was straining up, and a pair of baby arms was pulling, oh, *so* hard; and, in a sort of coma, big, pompous, grouchy Councilman Simpkins took that hanging ribbon! A band struck up a quick march, and round and round trod that happy, singing ring, with Old Bill looming up as big as a mountain amongst its foothills! Laugh? I thought His Honor would *burst!*

As that ribbon spiral got wound, Simpkins, coming back, said, with a growl:—

"I was afraid I would tramp on a kid or two in that silly stunt."

"It wasn't silly, Bill," said Gadsby. "It was *grand!"* And Tony Bandamita sang out:—

"Gooda work, Councilmanna! My four bambinos walka right in fronta you, and twista ribbons!"

Simpkins, though, would only snort, and pass on.

ON A WARM Sunday, Kathlyn and Julius, poking around in Branton Hills' suburbs, occasionally found an odd formation of fossilization, installing it amidst our Hall of Natural History's displays. Shortly following such an installation, a famous savant on volcanic activity noting a most propitious rock formation amongst Julius' groups, thought of cutting into it; for ordinary, most prosaic rocks *may* contain surprising information; and, upon arriving at Branton Hills' railway station, ran across old Pat Ryan, czar of its trunk room.

"Ah, my man! I want to find a lapidary."

"A what?"

"It isn't a 'what,' it's a lapidary."

"Lapidary, is it? Lapidary, lapidary, lapi—lapi—la—. No, I—"

Now this savant was in a hurry, and said, snappily:—

"But a city as big as Branton Hills *has a* lapidary, I trust!"

"Oh, Branton Hills has a lot of things. But, wait a bit! It ain't a lavatory what you want, is it?"

But at this instant, to old Pat's salvation, Kathlyn, passing by, said:—

"All right, Pat. I know about this;" and, both taking a taxi, old Pat walking round and round, scratching his bald crown, was murmuring:

"Lapid—Aho! I got it! It's probably a crittur up at that zoo! I ain't forgot that hop, skip and jump, walloping Australian tornado! And now His Honor has put in a lapidary!! I think I'll go up with that old canvas bag! But why all sich high-brow stuff in naming critturs? This lapidary thing might turn out only a rat, or a goofy bug!"

But that *fairy* bug, Dan Cupid, goofy or not, as you wish, was buzzing around again; and, though this story is not of wild, romantic infatuations, in which rival villains fight for a fair lady's hand, I am bound to say that Cupid has put on an act varying *much* from his works in Gadsby's mansion; for *this* arrow from his bow caught two young folks to whom a dollar bill was as long, broad and high as City Hall. Both had to work for a living; but by saving a bit, off and on, Sarah Young, who, you know, with Priscilla Standish first thought of our Night School, and Paul Johnson, who did odd jobs around town, such as caring for lawns, painting and "man-of-all-work," had put by a small bank account. Paul was an orphan, as was Sarah, who had grown up with a kindly old man, Tom Young; his "old woman," dying at about Sarah's fourth birthday. (That word "old woman, is common amongst Irish folks, and is not at all ungracious. It *had* to crawl into this story, through orthographical taboos, you know.) But Sarah, now a grown young lady, had that natural longing for a spot in which a woman might find that joy of living, in having "things to do for just us two" if bound by Cupid's gift—matrimony.

Many a day in passing that big church of Nancy's grand display, or Gadsby's rich mansion, Sarah had thought fondly about such things; for, as with any girl, marrying amidst blossoms, glamour and organ music was a goal, to attain which was actual bliss. But such rituals call for cash; and lots of it, too. Also, Old Tom Young had no room in any way fit for such an occasion.

So Sarah would walk past, possibly a bit sad, but looking forward to a coming happy day. And it wasn't so far off. My, no! As Nancy had thought April was "a million months long," Sarah's days swung past in a dizzy whirl; during which, in company with Paul on Saturday nights, a small thing or two was happily bought for that "Cupid's Coop," as both found a lot of fun in calling it. But Sarah naturally had girl chums, just as Nancy and Kathlyn had; for most of that old Organization was still in town; and many a gift found its way to this girl who, though poor in worldly goods, was as rich as old King Midas in a bright, happy disposition; for anybody who didn't know that magic captivation of Sarah Young's laugh, that rich crown of light, fluffy hair, or that grand, proud, upright walk, wasn't amongst Branton Hills' population. Paul, scratching around shady paths, a potato patch or two, front yards, back yards, and city parks, was known to many an old family man; who upon knowing of his coming variation in living conditions, thought way, way back to his own romantic youth; so Paul, going to Sarah at night, brought small but practical gifts for that "coop."

As Sarah and Paul stood in front of City Hall on a hot July night, Sarah scanning Branton Hills' "Post" for "vacant rooms," who should walk up but His Honor! And that kindly hand shot out with:—

"Aha! If it isn't Paul and Sarah! What's Sarah hunting for, Paul?"

"Sarah is looking for a room for us, sir.

"*Us?* Did you say 'us'? Oho! H-mmm! I'm on! How soon will you want it?"

"Oh," said Sarah, blushing, "not for about a month."

"But," said His Honor, "you shouldn't start out in a room. You would want from four to six, I should think."

Sarah, still ogling that "rooms" column, said, softly:—

"Four to six rooms? That's just grand if you can afford such. But,—

"Wait!" said Gadsby, who, taking Paul's and Sarah's arms, and strolling along, told of a small six-room bungalow of his, just around from Nancy's.

"And you two will pay just nothing a month for it. It's yours, from front porch to roof top, as a gift to two of my most loyal pals.

And instantly a copy of Branton Hills' "Post" was blowing across Broadway in a fluky July wind!

Now, as this young pair was to start out frugally, it wouldn't do to lay out too much for, as Sarah said, "about forty words by a pastor, and *a* kiss."

So only Priscilla stood up with Sarah; and Bill Gadsby, in all his sartorial glory, with Paul, in Parson Brown's small study; both girls in dainty morning clothing; Sarah carrying a bunch of gay nasturtiums, claiming that such warm, bright colorings would add as much charm to that short occasion as a thousand dollars' worth of orchids. Now, such girls as Sarah, with that capacity for finding satisfaction so simply, don't grow as abundantly as hollyhocks—and Paul found that Gadsby's old Organization was a group knowing what a dollar is: just a dollar.

OCCASIONALLY A SIGHT bobs up without warning in a city, which starts a train of thought, sad or gay, according to how you look at it. And so, Lucy, Priscilla, and Virginia Adams, walking along Broadway, saw a crowd around a lamp post, upon which was a patrol-box; and, though our girls don't customarily follow up such sights, Lucy saw a man's form sprawling flat up against that post, as limp as a rag. Priscilla said, in disgust:—

"*Ugh!!* It's Norman Antor! Drunk again!!" and Virginia, hastily grasping both girls' arms and hurrying past, said:—

"So!! His vacation in jail didn't do him any good! But, still, it's too bad. Norman is a good looking, manly lad, with a good mind and a thorough schooling. And *now* look at him! A *common drunk!!*'

Priscilla *was* sad, too, saying:—"Awful! Awful for so young a chap. What is his Dad doing now?"

"Still in jail," was all Virginia could say; adding sadly: "I do pity poor young Mary, who sold Antor's liquor, you know. Doris says that lots of school-girls snub that kid. Now that's not right. It's downright *horrid!* Mary was brought up in what you almost might call a pool of liquor. and I don't call it fair to snub a child for that; for you know that, not only 'Past' Councilman Antor, but also *Madam* Antor, got what our boys call 'litup' on many public occasions. Antor's pantry was *full* of it! Which way could that poor kid look without finding it? You know Mary is not so old as most of us; and I'm just going to *go* to that child and try to bring a ray of comfort into that young mind. That rum-guzzling Antor family!! *Ugh!!*"

~ ~ ~ ~ ~

BUT A CITY ALSO has amusing sights; and our trio ran plump into that kind, just around a turn; for, standing on a soap box, shouting a high-sounding jargon of rapidly shot words, was Arthur Rankin, an original Organization lad; a crowd of boys, a man or two, and a woman hanging laughingly around. Our trio's first inkling as to what it was all about was Arthur's bail to Priscilla:—

"Aha! Branton Hills' fair womanhood is now approaching!!"

Now if our trio didn't know Arthur so thoroughly, such girls might balk at this publicity. But Priscilla and Arthur had had many a "slapping match" long ago, arising from childhood's spats; Priscilla originally living on an adjoining lot, and was Arthur's "first girl;" which, according to his old Aunt Anna, "was just silly puppy stuff!" So nobody thought anything of this public hail and Arthur was raving on about "which puts an instant stop to all pain; will rid you of anything from dandruff to ingrowing nails; will build up a strong body from a puny runt; will grow hair on a billiard-ball scalp, and *taboo* it on a lady's chin; will put a glamorous gloss on tooth or nail; stop stomach growls; oil up kinky joints, and bring you to happy, smiling clays of Utopian bliss! How many, Priscilla? Only a dollar a box; two for dollar-sixty!"

Priscilla, laughing, said:—

"Not any today, thank you, Art! All I want is a pair of juicy lamb chops—a dish of onions—a dish of squash—a dish of carrots—a pint of milk—potato-chips—hot biscuits—cold slaw—custard pudding – nuts—raisins—"

"Whoa, Priscilla! Hop right up on this box! I know that word-slinging ability of old" and as that crowd was fading away, Priscilla said:

"This is odd work for you, Arthur; *you* so good a draughtsman. What's up?"

And Arthur, a happy, rollicking boy, having always had all such things as most boys had, with a Dad making good pay as a railroad conductor, told sadly of an awful railway smash-up which took "Dad" away from four small Rankin orphans, whom Arthur was now supporting; and a scarcity of jobs in Branton Hills and of trips to surrounding towns, always finding that old sign out: "No Work Today." Of this soap box opportunity bobbing up, which was now bringing in good cash. So our girls found that our Branton Hills boys didn't shirk work of any kind, if brought right up against want.

BUT WHAT ABOUT Branton Hills' municipal affairs, right now? In two months it was to ballot on who should sit in past-Councilman Antor's chair; and a campaign was on which was actually sizzling. And in what a contrast to our city's start! For it has grown rapidly; and, in comparison to that day upon which a thousand ballots was a big outpouring of popular clamor now many politicians had City Hall aspirations. And *who* do you think was running for Council, now? William Gadsby. Popularly known as Bill! Bill, Branton Hills' famous dandy; Bill, that consummation of all Branton Hills girls' most romantic wish; Bill, that "outdoor part" of Branton Hills' most aristocratic tailor shop! Naturally, opposing groups fought for that vacancy; part of our population clamoring loudly for Bill, but with many just as strongly against him. So it was:—

"Put Bill Gadsby in!! Bill has all our Mayor's good points! Bill will work for all that is upright and good!"

And also:—

"What! Bill Gadsby? Is this town plumb crazy? Say! If you put that fop in City Hall you'll find all its railings flapping with pink satin ribbons; a janitor at its main door, squirting vanilla on all who go in; and its front lawn will turn into a pansy farm! Put a *man* in City Hall, not a sissy who thinks out 'upsy-downsy, insy-outsy' camping suits for girls!"

But though this didn't annoy Bill, it *did* stir up Nancy, with:—

"Oh! That's just an abomination! *Such* talk about so grand a young chap! But I just saw a billboard with a sign saying: 'Bill Gadsby for Council;' so, probably I shouldn't worry, for Bill is as good as in."

"Baby," said Gadsby, kindly, "that's only a billboard, and billboards don't put a man in City Hall. It's *ballots,* darling; *thousands* of ballots, that fill Council chairs."

"But, Daddy, I'm going to root for Bill. I'll stand up on a stump, or in a tip-cart, or—"

"Whoa! Wait a bit!" and Gadsby sat down by his "baby girl," saying: "You can't go on a stumping campaign without knowing a lot about municipal affairs; which you don't. Any antagonist who knows about such things would out-talk you without half trying. No, darling, this political stuff is too big for you. You just look out for things in that small bungalow of yours, and allow Branton Hills to fight to put Bill in. You know my old slogan:—'Man at a city's front; woman at a cabin door.' "

And Nancy, fondly stroking his hand, said:

"Man at a city's front! What a grand post for a man! A city, a big, rushing, dashing, slamming, banging, boiling mass of humanity! A city; with its bright, happy, sunny parks; and its sad, dark slums; its rich mansions and its shanty-town shacks; its shops, inns, shows, courts, airports, railway stations, hospitals, schools, church groups, social clubs, and,—and,—*Oh! What* a magic visualization of human thought it is! But it is as a small child. It looks for a strong arm to support its first toddlings; for adult minds to pilot it around many pitfalls: and onward, *onward!!* To a shining goal!!" and Nancy's crown of rich brown hair sank lovingly in Gadsby's lap.

During this outburst Gadsby had sat dumb; but finally saying, proudly:—

"So, ho! My baby girl has grown up! Dolls and sand-digging tools don't call, as of old. And small, dirty paws, and a tiny smudgy chin, transform, almost in a twinkling into charming hands and a chin of maturity. My, my! It was but a month or two ago that you, in pig-tails and gingham—"

"No, Daddy! It was a *mighty long* month or two ago; and it's not pig-tails and gingham, now, but a husband and a baby."

"All right, kid; but as you grow old, you'll find that, in glancing backwards, months look mighty short; and small tots grow up, almost in a night. A month *from now* looks awfully far off: but *last month?* Pff! That was only last night!"

Thus did Nancy and His Honor talk, until a vigorous honking at his curb told of Frank, "looking for a cook," for it was six o'clock.

ANY MAN WITH so kindly a disposition toward Youth as has brought our Mayor forward in Branton Hills' history, may, without warning, run across an occasion which holds an opportunity for adding a bit of joy in living. So, as Gadsby stood, on a chilly fall day, in front of that big glass building which was built for a city florist, admiring a charming display of blossoming plants, a small girl, still in Grammar School. said, shyly:—

"Hulloa."

"Hulloa, you. School out?"

"On Saturdays, school is always out."

"That's so; it *is* Saturday, isn't it? Going in?"

"In!! My, no! *I* can't go into that fairyland!"

"No? Why not, pray?"

"Aw! I dunno; but nobody has took kids—"

"Took? Took? Say, young lady, you must study your grammar book. Branton Hills schools don't —"

"Uh-huh; I know. But a kid just can't—"

"By golly! A kid *can!* Grab my hand."

Now, many a fairy book has told, in glowing words, of childhood's joys and thrills at amazing sights; but *no* fairy book *could* show, in cold print, what Gadsby ran up against as that big door shut, and a child stood stock still—and *dumb!* Two small arms hung limply down, against a poor, oh, *so* poor skirt; and two big staring brown orbs took in that vision of floral glory, which is found in just that kind of a big glass building on a cold, raw autumn day.

Gadsby said not a word; slowly strolling down a path amidst thousands of gladioli; around a turn, and up a path, along which stood pots and pots of fuchsias, salvias and cannas; and to a cross-path, down which was a big flat pansy patch, tubs of blossoming lilacs, and stiff, straight carnations. Not a word from Gadsby, for his mind was on that small bunch of rapturous joy just in front of him. But, finally, just to pry a bit into that baby mind, His Honor said:—

"Looks kind of good, don't it?"

A tiny form shrunk down about an inch; and an also tiny bosom, rising and falling in a thralldom of bliss, finally put forth a long, long,—

"O-h-h-h-h!!

It was so long that Gadsby was in a quandary as to how such small lungs could hold it.

Now in watching this tot thrilling at its first visit to such a world of floral glory, Gadsby got what boys call "a hunch;" and said:—

"You don't find blossoms in your yard this month, *do* you?"

If you know childhood you know that thrills don't last long without a call for information. And Gadsby got such a call, with:—

"No, sir. Is this God's parlor?"

Now Gadsby wouldn't, for anything, spoil a childish thought; so said, kindly:—

"It's part of it. God's parlor is awfully big, you know."

"My parlor is awfully *small;* and not any bloss—Oh! Wouldn't God—?"

Gadsby's hunch was now working, full tilt; and so, as this loving family man, having had four kids of his own, and this tot from a poor family with its "awfully small" parlor,—had trod this big glass building's paths again and again; round and round, an almost monstrous sigh from an almost bursting tiny bosom, said, "I'll think of God's parlor, always and always and *always!!* and Gadsby, on glancing upwards, saw a distinct drooping and curving of many stalks; which is a plant's way of bowing to a child. And, at Branton Hills' following Council night a motion was—But I said Gadsby had a hunch. So, not only *this* school-girl's awfully small parlor, but many such throughout Branton Hills' poor districts, soon found a "big girl" from Gadsby's original Organization of Youth at its front door with plants from that big glass building, in which our City Florist works in God's parlor. (P.S. *Go* with a child to *your* City Florist's big glass building. It's a *duty!)*

I am now going back to my saying that a city has all kinds of goings-on; both sad and gay. So, as His Honor sat on his porch on a warm spring day, a paragraph in Branton Hills' "Post" brought forth such a vigorous *"Huh!"* that Lady Gadsby was curious, asking:—"What is it?"

So Gadsby said:—"What do you think of *this?* It says:—'In a wild swaying dash down Broadway last night at midnight, past—Councilman Antor's car hit a hydrant, killing him and Madam Antor instantly. Highway Patrolman Harry Grant, who was chasing that car in from our suburbs, says both horribly drunk, Antor grazing *four* cars, Madam shouting and singing wildly, with Grant arriving too tardily—to ward off that final crash."

Now Lady Gadsby was, first of all, a woman; and so got up quickly, saying:—

"Oh!! I must go down to poor young Mary, right *off,"* and Gadsby sat tapping his foot, saying:—

"So Antor's pantry probably still holds that stuff. Too bad. But, oh, that darling Mary! Just got into High School! Not long ago Lucy told us of girls snubbing that kid; but I trust that, from this horror, our Branton Hills girls will turn from snubbing to pity. This account says that Madam Antor also was drunk. A *woman* drunk!! And riding with a rum-sot man at a car's controls! *Woman!* From History's dawn, Man's soft, fond, loving pal! *Woman!* For whom wars of blood and agony cut Man down as you would mow a lawn! *Woman!* To whom infancy and childhood look for all that is upright and good! It's too bad; too bad!"

As in all such affairs you will always find two factions talking. Taking about what? Just now, about *Norman* Antor. What would this wiping out of his folks do to him? Norman was now living with Mary and two aunts who, coming from out of town, would try to plan for our two orphans; try to plan for Norman; Norman, brought up in a pool of liquor! Norman: tall, dark and manly and with a most ingratiating disposition if not drunk. But nobody could say. A group would claim that ''this fatality will bring him out of it;'' but his antagonists thought that "That guy will always drink."

A day or two from that crash, Nancy, coming into Gadsby's parlor, found Lucy talking with Lady Gadsby, Lucy asking:—

"Nancy, who is with young Mary Ardor now? That pair of aunts wouldn't stay, with all that liquor around."

"I just found out," said Nancy. "Mary is living with Old Lady Flanagan" and Lucy, though sad, had to laugh just a bit, saying:—

"Ha, ha! Old Lady Flanagan! What a *circus* I had trying to pry a zoo donation from that poor soul's skimpy funds! But, Nancy, Mary is in mighty good hands. That loving old Irish lady is a trump!"

ALONG IN APRIL, Gadsby sat finishing his morning toast as a boy, rushing in, put a "Post" on his lap *with a* wild, boyish gasp *of:—*

"My gosh, Mayor Gadsby, *Look!!"* and Gadsby saw a word about a foot high. It was W—A—R. Lady Gadsby saw it also, slowly sinking into a chair. At that instant both Nancy and Kathlyn burst frantically in, Nancy lugging Baby Lillian, now almost two, and a big load for so small a woman, Nancy gasping out:—

"Daddy!! Must Bill and Julius and Frank and John—"

Gadsby put down his "Post" and, pulling Nancy down onto his lap, said:—

"Nancy darling, Bill and Julius and Frank and John must. Old Glory is calling, baby, and no Branton Hills boy will balk at *that* call. It's awful, but it's a fact, now."

Lady Gadsby said nothing, but Nancy and Kathlyn saw an ashy pallor on that matronly brow; and Gadsby going out without waiting for his customary kiss.

For what you might call an instant, Branton Hills, in blank, black gloom, stood stock still. But not for long. Days got to flashing past, with that awful sight of girls, out to lunch, saying:—

"Four from our shop; and that big cotton mill has *forty-six* who will go."

With Virginia saying:—

"About all that our boys talk about is uniforms, pay, transportation, army corps, divisions, naval squadrons, and so on."

An occasional Branton Hills politician thought that it "might blow out in a month or two;" but your Historian knows that it didn't; all of that "blowing" consisting of blasts from that military clarion, calling for mobilization.

~ ~ ~ ~ ~

DAYS! DAYS! DAYS! Finally, on May Fourth, that day of tiny Nancy's big church ritual, you know; that day, upon which any woman would look back with romantic joy, Nancy, with Kathlyn, Lady Gadsby and His Honor, stood at Branton Hills' big railway station, at which our Municipal Band was drawn up; in back of which stood, in solid ranks, this city's grand young manhood, Bill, Julius, Frank, John, Paul and Norman standing just as straight and rigid as any. As that long, long troop train got its signal to start, - but you know all about such sights, going on daily, from our Pacific coast to Atlantic docks.

As it shot around a turn, and Gadsby was walking sadly toward City Hall, a Grammar School boy hurrying up to him said:—

"*Wow!! I wish I* could go to war!"

"Hi!" said Gadsby. "If it isn't Kid Banks!"

"Aw! Cut that kid stuff! I'm *Allan* Banks! Son of *Councilman* Banks!"

"Oh, pardon. But you don't want to go to war, boy."

"*Aw! I do too!!*"

"But young boys *can't* go to war."

86

"I know that; and I wish this will last until I grow so I *can* go. It's just grand! A big cannon says *Boom! Boom!* and,—"

"Sit down on this wall, boy. I want to talk to you."

"All right. Shoot!"

"Now look, Allan. If this war should last until you grow up, just think of how many *thousands* of troops it would kill. How many grand. good lads it would put right out of this world."

"Gosh! That's so, ain't it! I didn't think of guys dyin'."

"But a man *has* to think of that, Allan. And *you* will, as you grow up. My two big sons just put off on that big troop train. I don't know *how* long Bill and Julius will stay away. Your big cannon might go *Boom!* and hit Bill or Julius. Do you know Frank Morgan, Paul Johnson and John Smith? All right; that big cannon might hit that trio, too. Nobody can say *who* a cannon will hit, Allan. Now, you go right on through Grammar School, and grow up into a big strong man, and don't think about war;" and Gadsby, standing and gazing far off to Branton Hills' charming hill district, thought: "I think *that* will bust up a wild young ambition!"

But that kid, turning back, sang out:—

"Say!! If this scrap stops, and a *big* war *starts,—Aha,* boy! You just watch Allan Banks! Son of Councilman Banks!!" and a small fist was pounding viciously on an also small bosom.

"By golly!" said Gadsby, walking away, "that's Tomorrow talking!"

~ ~ ~ ~ ~

SO NOW THIS history will drift along; along through days and months; days and months of that awful gnawing doubt; actually a paradox, for it was a "conscious coma;" mornings on which Branton Hills' icy blood shrank from looking at our city's "Post," for its casualty list was rapidly—too rapidly,—growing. Days and days of our girlhood and womanhood rolling thousands of long, narrow cotton strips; packing loving gifts from many a pantry; Nancy and Kathlyn thinking constantly of Frank and John; Lucy almost down and out from worrying about Paul; Kathlyn knowing just how Julius is missing his Hall of Natural History, and how its staff is praying for him; Nancy's radio shut down tight, for so much as a thought of Station KBH was as a thrust of a sword. Days. Days. Days of shouting orators, blaring bands, troops from far away pausing at our big railway station, as girls, going through long trains of cars, took doughnuts and hot drinks. In Gadsby's parlor window hung that famous "World War flag" of nothing but stars; nobody knowing at what instant a *gold* star would show upon it. A star for Bill; a star for Julius. Ah, Bill! Branton Hills' fop! Bill Gadsby now in an ill-fitting and un-stylish khaki uniform.

Gadsby's mansion had no brilliant night lights, now; just his parlor lamp and a small light or two in hallways or on stairways. Only our Mayor and his Lady, now worrying, worrying, worrying; but both of good, staunch old Colonial stock; and "carrying on" with good old Plymouth Rock stability; and Nancy's baby, Lillian, too young to ask why Grandma "wasn't hungry," now; and didn't laugh so much.

Kathlyn got into our big hospital, this studious young lady's famous biological and microscopic ability holding out an opportunity for most practical work; for Branton Hills' shot-torn boys would soon start drifting in. And thus it was; with Lucy, Sarah and Virginia inspiring Branton Hills' womanhood to knit, knit, knit! You saw knitting on many a porch; knitting in railway trains; knitting during band music in City Park; knitting in shady arbors out at our big zoo; at many a woman's club,—*and,—actually,* knitting *in church!!* Finally a big factory, down by our railway station, put out a call for "anybody, man or woman, who wants to work on munitions;" and many a dainty Branton Hills girl sat at big, unfamiliar stamping, punching, grinding, or polishing outfits; tiring frail young backs and straining soft young hands; knowing that this factory's output might—and probably would,—rob a woman across that big Atlantic of a husband or son,—but, still, it is war!

Gadsby, smoking on his ivy-clad porch, as his Lady was industriously knitting, said, in a sort of soliloquy:—

"War! That awful condition which a famous military man in command of a division, long ago, said was synonymous with Satan and all his cohorts! War! That awful condition of human minds coming down from *way, way* back of all history; that vast void during which sympathy was not known; during which animals fought with tooth, claw or horn; that vast void during which wounds had no soothing balm, until thirst, agony or a final swoon laid low a gigantic mammoth, or a tiny, gasping fawn! But now, again, in this grand day of Man's magically growing brain, this day of kindly crooning to infants in cribs; kindly talks to boys and girls in school; and blood-tingling orations from thousands of pulpits upon that Holy Command: 'Thou Shalt Not Kill,' now, *again,* Man is out to kill his own kind." And Lady Gadsby could only sigh.

AS THIS STORY has shown, *Youth,* if adults will only admit that it has any brains at all, will stand out, today, in a most promising light. Philosophically, Youth is Wisdom in formation, and with many thoughts startling to adult minds; and, industrially, this vast World's coining stability is now, *today,* in its bands; growing slowly, as a blossom grows from its bud. If you will furnish him with a thorough schooling, you can plank down your dollar that Youth, *starting out* from this miraculous day, will not lag nor shirk on that *coming* day in which old joints, rusty and crackling, must slow down; and, calling for an oil can, you will find that Youth *only,* is that lubrication which can run Tomorrow's World. But Youth must not go thinking that all its plans will turn out all right; and young Marian Hopkins found this out. Marian, you know, took part in our airport initiation. But Marian, only a kid at that day, has grown up—or half-way up, anyway, and just graduating from Grammar School; upon which big day a child "knows" as much as any famous savant of antiquity! But, as this story runs in skips and jumps, strict chronological continuity is not a possibility. So, Marian is now half grown up. Now that big airport, as you also know, was just back of Marian's back yard; and as that yard was much too big for anything that Marian's Dad could do with it, it was put up for disposal. But nobody would go to look at it; to say nothing of buying it. But Old Bill Simpkins, past antagonist of Gadsby's Organization of Youth, did go out to look at it; but said, with his customary growl

"Too many aircraft always roaring and zooming. Too far out of town. And you ask too much for it, anyway.

But Marian thought that Branton Hills, as a municipality, should own it; figuring that that airport would grow, and that yard was practically a part of it, anyway. So Marian, going to His Honor, as about anybody in town did, without an instant's dallying, "told him," (!) what his Council should do.

"But," said Gadsby, "what a City Council should do, and what it *will* do, don't always match up.

"Can't I go and talk to it?"

"What! To our Council? No; that is, not as a body. But if you can run across a Councilman out of City Hall you can say what you wish. A Councilman is just an ordinary man, you know." But a Councilman out

of City Hall was a hard man to find; and a child couldn't go to a man's mansion to "talk him around." But, by grand luck, in a month or so, Marian did find, and *win,* all but Simpkins.

On Council night, Simpkins took up a good,—or I should say, bad— half hour against Branton Hills "buying any old dump or scrap land that is.

What this city put up. Was coming to?" and so on, and so on. And Marian's back yard wasn't bought. Now Youth is all right if you rub its fur in a way which suits it; but, man!! hold on to your hat, if you don't!! And Marian's fur was all lumpy. *Boy! was that kid MAD!!*

Now, just by luck, March thirty-first, coming along as days do, you know, found Marian in front of a toy shop window, in which, way down front, was a box of cigars, with a card saying:

"This Brand Will Start His Blood Tingling." And Marian, as boys say, was "on" in an instant; and bought a cigar. Not a box, not a bunch, but just a cigar. Coming out Marian saw His Honor and Simpkins passing; Simpkins saying:—

"All right. I'll drop around, tonight." And was Marian happy? Wait a bit.

That night as Gadsby and Simpkins sat talking in His Honor's parlor, who would, "just by luck," (??) walk in, but Marian; saying, oh, *so* shyly:—

"Just thought I'd drop in to chat with Nancy," and, on passing a couch, slyly laid that cigar on it. Now Simpkins, in addition to his famous grouch, was a parsimonious old crab; who, though drawing good pay as Councilman, couldn't pass up anything that cost nothing; and, in gazing around, saw that cigar; and, with a big apologizing yawn, and slinking onto that couch as a cat slinks up on a bird, and, oh, *so* nonchalantly lighting a match, was soon puffing away and raving about Branton Hills politics. Out in a back parlor sat Marian and Nancy on a big divan, hugging tightly up, arm in arm, and almost suffocating from holding back youthful anticipations, as Simpkins said:—

" … and that Hopkins back yard stunt! Ridiculous! Why, his kid was out, trying to find all of our Council to talk it into buying. Bah! And *did* I block it? I'll say I did! You don't find kids today laughing at Councilman Simpkins."

An actual *spasm* of giggling in that back parlor had Gadsby looking around, inquiringly.

"No, sir!" Simpkins said. "No kid can fool Coun—"

BANG!!

Gadsby, jumping up *saw* only a frazzly cigar stump in Old Bill's mouth, as that palpitating individual was vigorously brushing off falling sparks as His Honor's rugs got a rain of tobacco scraps! Gadsby was "on" in an instant, noticing Marian and Nancy rolling and tumbling around on that big divan, and doubling up in a giggling fit, way out of control. Finally Simpkins angrily got up, viciously jamming on his tall silk hat; and Marian, fighting that giggling fit, just *had* to call out:—

"*April Fool,* Councilman Simpkins!"

(And Mayor Gadsby, on a following Council night, got Marian's land bill through; many a Councilman holding his hand in front of his grinning mouth, in voting for bright, vitalic Youth.)

WIDOW ADAMS was sitting up again, for it was way past midnight, and Virginia was out. Many months ago Virginia was also out, and was brought back, unconscious. So now Nina was again sitting up, for Virginia was not a night-owl sort of a girl. Finally, around two o'clock, Nina couldn't stand it, and had to call in a passing patrolman. Now this patrolman was an original Organization of Youth boy, and had always known Nina and Virginia; and said:—

"Oh, now! I wouldn't worry so. Possibly a bus had a blowout; or—"

"*But* Virginia said nothing *about* going on a bus! Oh!! *How* could that child vanish so?"

Naturally, all that that patrolman could do was to call his station; and Nina, almost all in, lay down, until, just about dawn a jangling ringing brought this half wild woman to a front hall, shouting:—

"This is Nina Adams talking! Who? *What?* Virginia, is that you? What's wrong? What! You and Harold Thompson? Our aviator? You did what? Took his aircraft to *what* city? 'Why, that's so far you can't—" but Virginia had hung up.

So Nina also hung up, and sat down with a big, long sigh:—

"My Virginia, not *running* away, but flying away, to marry! Oh, this Youth of today!"

~ ~ ~ ~ ~

AROUND SIX O'CLOCK that night, Virginia and Harold stood arm in arm in Nina's parlor, as a big bus was groaning noisily away.

"But, Mama," said Virginia, sobbing pitifully, "I didn't think you would—"

"That's just it, Virginia, you *didn't* think!! But you *should!* How could *I* know what was going on? That's just you young folks of today. You think of nothing but your own silly, foolish doings, and you allow us old *good-for-nothings* to go crazy with worry!!" and Nina sank in a gasping swoon onto a sofa.

But old Doc Wilkins, arriving at Virginia's frantic call, knowing Nina's iron constitution from childhood, soon had that limp form back to normal; and, with a dark, disapproving scowl at Virginia. said:—

"Bring in a good batch of hot food, and your Ma will turn out all right," and going out, with a snort of disgust, and banging viciously that big front door!

Awful tidings in our Branton Hills' "Post," had so wrought up our ordinarily happy, laughing Sarah, who, with Paul abroad, was back, living again with old Tom Young, that Sarah, sitting on a low stool by old Tom's rocking chair was so still that Tom put down his "Post," saying:—

"Gift of gab all run out, kid?"

But Sarah had an odd, thoughtful look. Sarah's bosom was rising and falling abnormally; but, finally, looking quickly up at old Tom, Sarah said:—

"Daddy, I want to go to war."

"Do what?" If Sarah had said anything about jumping out of a balloon, or of buying a gorilla to play with, Tom Young wouldn't know any such astounding doubt as brought his rocking chair to a quick standstill.

"War? What kind of talk is this? A girl going to war? What for? How? *Say!!* Who *put* this crazy stunt into your brain, anyway?"

As you know, Sarah was not only charming in ways, but also in build; and, with that glorious crown of brownish-gold hair, that always smiling mouth and that soft, plump girlishly-girlish form, no man, Tom Young nor anybody, could think of Sarah and war in a solitary thought. So Sarah said, softly:—

"Last night, our Night School trio thought that our boys, so far away, must miss us, and Branton Hills sights; and Doris said, 'Branton Hills sounds.' And so, why couldn't our trio join that big group of musicians which is sailing soon? And, Daddy, you know Paul is in that army. I don't know that I could find him, but- but- but I want to try. And Kathlyn is talking of going as biologist with a big hospital unit; so possibly I could stay with it."

Tom Young was *dumb!* His "Post" actually *had* told of such a musical outfit about to sail; but it was a man's organization. So, now it has got around to *this!* Our girls, our dainty, loving girls, brimful of both sympathy and patriotism, wanting to go into that tough, laborious work of singing in army camps; in huts; in hospitals; singing from trucks rolling along country roads along which sat platoons and battalions of troops, waiting for word which might bring to this or that boy his last long gun-toting tramp. Singing in—"*Aw,* darling! Your trio was fooling, wasn't it? Now, girls don't –"

"Daddy, girls *do!* So, if our folks don't put up too much of a—"

"Aha."! Now you said a mouthful; *if* your folks *don't!* Darling, I'll say just two words as my part in this crazy stunt: *'Nothing doing'!!* Kathlyn's work is mighty important; singing isn't."

Sarah had not grown up from infancy in kindly Tom's cabin without knowing that his no was a "no!!" and not a flimsy, hollow word which a whining, or a sniffling, or a bawling child could switch around into: "Oh, all right, if you want to." So Sarah still sat on that low stool; or, to turn it around almost backwards,—Sarah sat on that stool,—still. So still that Tom's old tin clock on its wall hooks was soon dominating that small room with its rhythmic ticking, as a conductor's baton controls a brass band's pianissimos. Finally Sarah said softly, slowly, sadly and with a big, big sigh:—

"I did so want to go." And that small clock was ticking, ticking, ticking....

For a full hour Sarah and old Tom sat talking and rocking, until Sarah, phoning to Doris, said:—"My Dad says no."

And Doris, phoning back to Sarah, said:—"So did my Dad."

And, as Virginia Adams was that trio's third part; and as Sarah and Doris had always known Nina Adams' strong will; and as,—Oh, hum! It was a happy fascination until adult minds got hold of it!

GADSBY WAS WALKING back from a visit down in Branton Hills' manufacturing district on a Saturday night. A busy day's traffic had had its noisy run; and with not many folks in sight, His Honor got along without having to stop to grasp a hand, or talk; for a Mayor out of City Hall is a shining mark for any politician. And so, coming to

Broadway, a booming bass drum and sounds of singing, told of a small Salvation Army unit carrying on amidst Broadway's night shopping crowds. Gadsby, walking toward that group, saw a young girl, back towards him, just finishing a long, soulful oration, saying:—

"... and I can say this to you, for I know what I am talking about; for I was brought up in *a pool of liquor!!*"

As that army group was starting to march on, with this girl turning towards Gadsby, His Honor had to gasp, astonishingly:—

"Why! Mary Antor!!"

"Oh! If it isn't Mayor Gadsby! I don't run across you much, now-a-days. How is Lady Gadsby holding up during this awful war?"

All such family gossip passing quickly, Gadsby said:—

"But this Salvation Army work, Mary? How long—"

Mary and His Honor had to walk along, as that big drum was now pounding a block away. During that walk Gadsby found out all about that vast void in Mary's bungalow following that fatal auto crash; and all about "two old maid aunts" as Mary said, who had all that pantry's liquor thrown down a drain and got cut, also, a day or two following; all about living now at Old Lady Flanagan's.

"...for I just *couldn't* stay in that bungalow, with nobody around, you know." And all about loving companionship in that grand old lady's arms; and of Mary's finding that Flanagan, who got such a wallop from Antor's killing, wasn't drinking so much, now which put it into Mary's mind that many a man would, with kindly coaching, turn from it.

"And I think that my nightly talks against liquor, hit; and hit *hard,* too; for almost nightly a poor down-and-out will follow along with our band, promising to cut it out and go straight. *Oh, why* didn't I try to stop Norman's drinking?"

"Probably," said Gadsby, "you did, in your girlish way; but you know boys don't think that small girls know anything. I'd put up any amount that Norman, in that far-away camp, is thinking of you, constantly."

"Oh-h-h-h! If I could only *know* that I" and a look of almost sanctity, and a big, long-drawn sigh told what a turmoil was going on in this young girl's mind. "But I'm going on, and on and on with this night talking until Norman is back again. Possibly a plan will turn up toward both of us living down our past,—and our sorrow." And Gadsby, slowly plodding along towards his dimly lit mansion, thought of a slight transposition of that scriptural quotation: "And your sins, you adults, shall fall upon your offspring, unto your third and fourth—"

"Oh, if a man would only think of his offspring having to carry on, long past his last day! And of how hard it is for a boy or girl to stand up and proudly (?) claim that so-and-so 'was my Dad,' if all Branton Hills knows of that Dad's inglorious past. Poor kids!" for you know that Gadsby said, in this story's start, that "a man should so carry on his daily affairs as to bring no word of admonition from anybody;" for a man's doings should put a stain upon no soul but his own.

But, *aha!!* As His Honor got to his parlor, his sad mind found a happy, smiling Lady awaiting him; crying joyously:—

"Look! Look, John! Word from William! From Bill, in Paris!"

Bill's first communication said:—

"Darling Folks: Julius and I just got into this town from a month of hard marching, ditch-digging and fighting. I am all right, and so is Julius. Ran across Frank, who is on duty at our Commissary. Lucky guy! Lots of food always around! Paul is growing fat. Looks mighty good. Oh, how all of us do miss you and good old Branton Hills! I can't find a solitary suit in this town that I would put on to go to a dog fight! *Such fashion!*" and so on; just a natural outpouring from a boy, away on his first trip from his Dad's kindly roof.

"Ha, ha!" said Gadsby, laughing jovially; "That's our Bill, all right! Always thinking of dolling *up!*" and Lady Gadsby, rising quickly, said:—

"Oh, I must call up Nancy, Kathlyn and Sarah!" and, in a trio of small bungalows, joy, *wild* joy, found its way into girlish minds!

As Gadsby sat, going through this good word again and again, a mirthful chuckling had Lady Gadsby asking:—

"What's so funny about it?"

"Nothing; only if I didn't know that Frank is such a grand, good lad, I'd think Bill was hiding *a* bit from us; for that 'on duty at Commissary' *might* amount only to potato paring!"

PRISCILLA STANDISH was waiting at our big railroad station, on a warm Spring day, for a train to pull out, so that cross-track traffic could start again. It *was* just an ordinary train such as stop hourly at Branton Hills, but Priscilla saw that a group was hurrying toward a combination-car, way up forward. Now Priscilla was not a girl who found morbid curiosity in any such a public spot; but, still, an odd, uncanny sort of thrill,—almost a chill, in fact,—was urging, urging a slow walk toward that car. Just why, Priscilla didn't know; but such things do occur in a human mind. So Priscilla soon was standing on a trunk truck, gazing down into that group which now was slowly moving back, forming room for taking out a young man in khaki uniform, on a hospital cot. With a gasp of horror, Priscilla was instantly down from that truck, pushing through that group, and crying out, wildly:—

"*Arthur!* Arthur Rankin! Oh! Oh! What is it, darling?" and looking up at a hospital assistant, "Is it bad?"

"Don't know, right now, lady," said that snowy clad official. "Unconscious. But our big hospital will do all it can for him."

Arthur Rankin! Arthur, with whom Priscilla had had many a childhood spat! Arthur who had shown that "puppy stuff" for Priscilla, that his old aunt was always so disapprovingly sniffing at! And now, unconscious on a,—

With a murmuring of sympathy from that sorrowing public, now dissolving, as all crowds do, Priscilla had a quick, comforting thought: "Kathlyn is working at that hospital!"

Kathlyn had known Arthur as long as Priscilla had; and Kathlyn's famous ability would—

So our panting and worrying girl was hurrying along through Broadway's turning and inquiring crowds to that big hospital which our Organization of Youth had had built. And now Arthur was going, for not long, possibly, but, still possibly for—

~ ~ ~ ~ ~

IT WAS MIDNIGHT in that big still building. Old Doctor Wilkins stood by Arthur's cot; Priscilla, sobbing pitifully, was waiting in a corridor, with Lady Standish giving what comfort a woman could. Lady Standish, who took in dogs, cats, rabbits or any living thing that was hurt, sick or lost; Lady Standish, donor of four thousand dollars for our big Zoo; Lady Standish, kindly savior of Clancy's and Dowd's "Big Four," now waiting, without ability to aid a *human* animal. Finally, Doctor Wilkins, coming out, said:—

"Kathlyn says no sign of blood contamination, but vitality low; *badly* low; sinking, I think. Railroad trip almost too much for him. Looks bad."

But, at this instant, an assistant, calling Wilkins, said Arthur was coming out of his coma; and was murmuring "about a woman known as Priscilla. Do you know anybody by—?"

With a racking sob, Priscilla shot through that door, Lady Standish quickly following. Arthur, picking up, a bit, from Priscilla's soft, oh, *so* soft and loving crooning and patting, took that fond hand and—sank back! Doctor Wilkins, looking knowingly at Priscilla, said:—

"If it is as I think, you two had had thoughts of—"

A vigorous nod from Priscilla, and an approving look from Lady Standish, and Doctor Wilkins said:—

"Hm-m-m! It should occur *right now!* Or,—"

As quick as a flash that snowy-clad assistant was phoning; and, *astonishingly* soon, our good Pastor Brown stood by that cot; and, with Arthur in a most surprising pick-up, holding Priscilla's hot, shaking hand, through that still hospital room was wafting Priscilla's soft, low words:—

"...you for my lawful husband, *until...* "

~ ~ ~ ~ ~

DOCTOR WILKINS, going out with Priscilla, now trying, oh, *so* hard for control; with grand, charming, loving Kathlyn, arm in arm, said:—

"That joy will pull him through. Boys, at war, so far *away,* will naturally droop, both in body and mind, from lack of a particular girl's snuggling and cuddling. So just wait until Kathlyn finds out all about his condition; and good food, with this happy culmination of a childhood infatuation, will put him in first-class condition, if no complications show up.

Ah! What an important part of a city's institutions a hospital is! What a comfort to all, to know that, should injury or any ailing condition of man, woman or child occur without warning, anybody can, simply through phoning find quick transportation at his door; and, with angrily clanging gongs, or high-pitch whistlings obtaining a "right of way" through all traffic, that institution's doors will swing apart, assistants will quickly surround that cot, and an ability for doing anything that Man *can* do is at hand. You know, almost daily, of capitalists of philanthropic mold, donating vast sums to a town or an association; but, in your historian's mind, no donation can do so much good as that which

builds, or maintains hospitalization for all. A library, a school, a boys'
or girls' club, a vacation facility, a "chair" of this or that in an institution of instruction,—all do much to build up a community. Both
doctoring as a study for a young man, and nursing for a girl form most
important parts of Mankind's activity.

And so, *just* four months from that *awful,* but also happy day, Arthur
Rankin sat in a hammock with Priscilla, on Lady Standish's porch, with
four small Rankins playing around; or was walking around that back
yard full of cats, dogs, rabbits, and so on, with no thought of soap box
orations in his mind.

ON A GRAND AUTUMN morning Branton Hills' "Post" boys ran
shouting down Broadway, showing in half-foot wording:
"FIGHTING STOPS!! HISTORY'S MOST DISASTROUS WAR IS
HISTORY NOW!!!" and again, Branton Hills stood stock still. But
only for an instant; for soon, it was, in all minds:—
"Thank God!! Oh, *ring* your loud church clarions! *Blow* your factory
blasts! Shout! Cry! Sing! *Play,* you bands! Burst your drums! Crack
your cymbals!"

Ah, what a sight on Broadway! Shop girls pouring out! Shop janitors
boarding up big glass windows against a surging mob! And, (sh-h-h-h)
many a church having in its still sanctity a woman or girl at its altar
rail.

Months, months, months! Branton Hills was again at its big railroad
station, its Municipal Band playing our grand National air, as a long
troop train, a solid mass of bunting, was snorting noisily in. And,
amidst that outpouring flood of Branton Hills boys, Lady Gadsby,
Nancy, Kathlyn and His Honor found Bill, Julius, Frank and John.
Sarah was just "going all apart" in Paul's arms, with Virginia swooning
in Harold's.

On old Lady Flanagan's porch sat Mary Antor; for, having had no
word from Norman for months, this grand young Salvation Army lass
was in sad, sad doubt. But soon, as that shouting mob was drifting
away, and happy family groups walking citywards, a khaki-clad lad,
hurrying to old Lady Flanagan's cabin, and jumping that low, ivy-clad
wall, had Mary, sobbing and laughing, in his arms. No. It wasn't Norman.

A CROWD WAS STANDING around in City Park, for a baby was missing. Patrol cars roaring around Branton Hills; many a woman hunting around through sympathy; kidnapping rumors flying around. His Honor was out of town; but on landing at our railroad station, and finding patrol cars drawn up at City Park, saw, in that crowd's midst, a tiny girl, of about six, with a bunch of big shouting officials, asking:—

"Who took that baby?"

"Did you do it?"

"Which way did it go?"

"How long ago did you miss it?"

"Say, kiddo!! *Why don't you talk?*"

An adult brain can stand a lot of such shouting, but a baby's is not in that class; so, totally dumb, and shaking with fright, this tot stood, thumb in mouth, and two big brown baby orbs just starting to grow moist, as His Honor, pushing in, said:—

"Wait a bit!!" and that bunch in uniform, knowing him, got up and Gadsby sat down on a rock, saying:—

"You can't find out a *thing* from a young child by such hard, gruff ways. This tiny lady is almost in a slump. Now, just start this crowd moving. I know a bit about Youth."

"That's right," said a big, husky patrolman. "If anybody living knows kids, it's you, sir."

So, as things got around to normal, His Honor, now sitting flat on City Park's smooth lawn, said, jovially:—

"Hulloa."

A big gulping sob in a tiny bosom—didn't gulp; and a grin ran around a small mouth, as our young lady said:—

"*So* many big cops! O-o-o! I got afraid!"

"I know, darling; but no big cops will shout at you now. *I* don't shout at tiny girls, do I?"

"No, sir; but if folks do shout, I go all woozy."

"*Woozy?* Woozy? Ha, ha! I'll look that up in a big book. But what's all this fuss about? Is it about a baby?"

A vigorous nodding of a bunch of brown curls.

"What? Fussing about a baby? A baby is too small to fuss about."

"O-o-o-o! It *isn't!!*"

"No?"

"No, sir. I fuss about my dolly, an' it's not half so big as a baby."

"That's so. Girls do fuss about dolls. My girls did."

"How many dolls has your girls got?"

"Ha, ha! Not any, now. My girls all got grown up and big."

During this calm, happy talk, a patrolman, coming up, said:—

"Shall I stick around, Your Honor? Any kidnapping facts?"

"I don't know, just now. Wait around about an hour, and drop in again."

So His Honor, Mayor of Branton Hills, and Childhood sat on that grassy lawn; a tiny tot making daisy chains, grass rings, and thrilling at Gadsby's story of how a boy, known as Jack, had to climb a big, big tall stalk to kill an awfully ugly giant. Finally Gadsby said:—

"I thought you had a baby playing with you."

"I did."

"Huh, it isn't playing now. Did it fly away?"

"Oho! No! A baby can't fly!"

"No. That's right. But how *could* a baby go away from you without your knowing it?"

"It didn't. I did know it."

Now, many may think that His Honor would thrill at this information; but Gadsby didn't. So, "playing around" for a bit, His Honor finally said:—

"I wish *I* had a baby to play with, right now!"

"*You* can."

"Can I? How?"

With a tiny hand on baby lips, our small lady said:—

"Go look in that lilac arbor; but *go soft!* I think it's snoozing."

And Gadsby, going to that arbor, got a frightful shock; for it was Lillian, Nancy's baby! Not having known of this "kidnapping" as his family couldn't find him by phoning, it *was* a shock; for His Honor was thinking of that young woman collapsing. So, upon that patrolman coming back, as told, Gadsby said:—

"Go and call up your station, *quickly!* Say that I want your Captain to notify my folks that Lillian is all right."

"Good gosh, Your Honor!! Is this tot your grandchild?"

"Grandchild or no grandchild, *you dash to that box!!*"

And so, again, John Gadsby, Champion of Youth, had shown officialdom that a child's brain and that of an adult vary as do a gigantic oak and its tiny acorn.

MOST OF GADSBY'S old Organization of Youth was still in town, though, as you know, grown up. So, on a Spring day, all of its forty boys and as many girls got most mystifying cards, saying:—

"Kindly go to Lilac Hill on May sixth, at four o'clock. IMPORTANT! IMPORTANT! IMPORTANT" That was all. Not a word to show its origin. No handwriting. Just a small, plain card in ordinary printing.

Not only that old Organization, but His Honor, Lady Gadsby, Old Tom Young, Tom Donaldson, Nina Adams, Lady Standish and Old Lady Flanagan got that odd card.

"Arrah! Phwat's this, anny *way?*" sang out that good old lady. "Is it court summons, a picnic, or a land auction? By gorry, it looks phony!"

Old Tom Young, in his rocking chair, said:—

"A card to go to Lilac Hill. It says 'important.' Ah! This Youth of to-day! I'll Put up a dollar that I can sniff a rat in this. But my girl is all right so I'll go."

And so it was, all around town. Nobody could fathom it.

Lilac Hill was as charming a spot as any that our big City Park could boast. Though known as a hill, it was but a slight knoll with surroundings of lilac shrubs, which, in May would always show a riot of bloom; this knoll sloping down to a pond, with islands, boats and aquatic plants. Lilac Hill had known many a picnic and similar outings; for Branton Hills folks, living for six days amidst bricks and asphalt, just *had* to go out on Sundays to this dainty knoll, living for an hour or so amongst its birds, blossoms and calm surroundings. City traffic was far away, only a faint rumbling coming to this natural sanctuary; and many a mind. and many a worn body had found a balm in its charms.

But that mystifying card! From whom was it? What was it? *Why* was it? "Oh, hum! Why rack brains by digging into it?" was Branton Hills' popular thought. "But, go and find out!" That, also, was our Organization's thought as May sixth was approaching.

"My gracious!" said Nancy. "It sounds actually spooky!"

But calm, practical Kathlyn said:—

"Spooks don't hop around in daylight."

May sixth had just that warm and balmy air that allows girls to put on flimsy, dainty things, and youths to don sports outfits; and His Honor, as that mystifying day was not far off, said:—

"This, I think, is a trick by a kid or two, to show us old ducks that an 'incog' can hold out, right up to its actual consummation. I don't know a thing about what's going on; but, by golly! I'll show up; and if any fun is afloat, I'll join in, full blast."

But!!—As our Organization boys and girls, and Branton Hills folks got to Lilac Hill, *not* a *thing was found* giving any indication that anything out of ordinary was to occur! Just that calm, charming knoll, with its lilacs, oaks, and happy vista out across Branton Hills' hill districts! What's this, anyway? A hoax? But all sat down, talking in a big group, until, at just four o'clock,—*look!* A stir, out back of that island boat landing! What? On that *pond?* This card said Lilac *Hill!* But I said that a stir was occurring in back of that boat landing, with its small shack for storing oars and such. If our big crowd was laughing and talking up to now, it quit! And quit mighty quickly, too! If you want to hold a crowd, just mystify it. Old Lady Flanagan was starting to shout about "this phony stuff," but Old Man Flanagan said:—

"Shut up! You ain't part of this show!"

Nancy was actually hopping up and down, but Kathlyn stood calmly watching; for this studious girl, *way* up in an "ology" or two, knows that, by slow, thoughtful watching, you can gain much, as against working up a wild, panicky condition.

Lady Gadsby said again and again: "What *is* going on?" but Nina Adams said: "You ought to know that today, anything can—"

But *look again!!* From in back of that boat landing, a big fairy float is coming! Slowly,—slowly—slowly; a cabin amidships, just *dripping* with lilacs, as still and noncommittal as old Gibraltar. Slowly, on and on it is coming; finally stopping right at that spot upon which our group is standing; forty boys, forty girls, and a big mob, all as still as a church. What *is* it, anyway? Is anybody in it? Not a sign of it. But wait! Aha! It *has* an occupant, for, coming out of that lilac glory *is - Parson Brown!!* Parson Brown? *What* was Parson Brown in that cabin for? Aha!! A lilac spray is moving; and, as our groups stand stock still, *look!* Lucy Donaldson is coming out! Oh! *What* a vision of girlish joy and glory!! And—and—and, ah! That lilac spray is moving again! Hulloa! Bill Gadsby is coming out!!

A Spring sun was slowly approaching its horizonward droop, shooting rays of gold down onto our gasping crowd, as Parson Brown said:—

"William Gadsby, do you ...?"

William, but shortly back from abroad, you know, standing with grand, military rigidity, said:

"I do."

"And Lucy Donaldson, do you ...?"

It didn't last long. Just a word or two; a burst of music of a famous march by John Smith, Branton Hills' organist, in that cabin with a small piano; just a—But that crowd couldn't wait for that! With a whoop His Honor sprang into that pond, wading swiftly to board that fairy craft; and in an instant Nancy was following him, splashing frantically along, and scrambling aboard to almost floor Bill with a gigantic hug as His Honor shook Bill's hand, with a loving arm about Lucy. Old Lady Flanagan was shouting wildly:—"Whoops! Whoops! By gorra! This young gang of today is a smart boonch!" and His Honor said:—

"Ha, ha! I didn't know a thing about this! Bill's a smart chap!" And Old Tom Donaldson, grabbing happy, laughing, blushing, palpitating Lucy as soon as that young lady was on dry land, said:—

"Say! You sly young chick! Why didn't you notify your old Dad?"

"Why, Daddy! That would spoil all my fun!!"

GADSBY, CLANCY and Dowd "just had" to, according to unanimous opinion, go out to Lady Standish's suburban plot of ground to visit "Big Four;" Gadsby, owing to an inborn liking for all animals; Clancy and Dowd from fond association with this particular group. It was a glorious spot; high, rolling land, with a patch of cool, shady woods, and a grand vista across hill and plain, with shining ponds and rich farm lands. And did "Big Four" *know* Clancy and Dowd? I'll say so! And soon, with much happy whinnying and "acting up," with two big roans poking inquiring snouts in Clancy's hands, and two big blacks snuggling Gadsby and Dowd, as happy a group of Man and animals as you could wish for, was soon accompanying Lady Standish around that vast patch.

Anything that such animals could want was at hand. A bright, sparkling brook was gabbling and gurgling through a stony gully, or dropping, with many brilliant rainbows, down a tiny fall.

"Sally," said Gadsby, "you do a grand work in maintaining this spot. If Mankind, as a body, would only think as you do, that an animal has a brain, and knows good living conditions, you wouldn't find so many poor, scraggly old Dobbins plodding around our towns, dragging a cart far too big; and with a man totally without sympathy on it."

And Lady Standish said:—

"I just *can't* think of anybody abusing an animal; nor of allowing it to stay around, sick, hurt or hungry. I think that an animal is but a point short of human; and, having a skin varying but slightly from our own, will know as much pain from a whipping as would a human child. A blow upon any animal, if I am within sight, is almost as a blow upon my own body. You would think that, with that vast gap which Mankind is continually placing back of him in his onward march in improving this big world, Man would think, a bit, of his pals of hoof, horn and claw. But I am glad to say that, in this country, laws in many a community admit that an animal has rights. Oh, how an animal that is hurt looks up at you, John! An animal's actions can inform you if it is in pain. It don't hop and jump around as usual. No. You find a sad, crouching, cringing, small bunch of fur or hair, whining, and plainly asking you to aid it. It isn't hard to find out what is wrong, John; any man or woman who would pass by such a sight, just isn't worth knowing. I just can't withstand it! Why, I think that not only animals, but plants can know pain. I carry a drink to many a poor, thirsty growing thing; or, if it is torn up I put it kindly back, and fix its soil up as comfortably as I can. *Anything* that is living, John, is worthy of Man's aid."

POOR OLD BILL Simpkins! Nothing in this world was worth anything; nobody was right; all wrong, all wrong! Simpkins had no kin; and, not marrying, was "just plodding along," living in a small room, with no fun, no constant company, no social goal to which to look forward; and had, thus, grown into what boys call "a big, old grouch." But it wasn't all Simpkins' fault. A human mind *was* built for contact with similar minds. It should,—in fact,—it *must* think about what is going on around it; for, if it is shut up in a thick, dark, bony box of a skull, it will always stay in that condition known as status quo; and grow up, antagonistic to all surroundings. But Simpkins didn't *want* to growl and grunt. It was practically as annoying to him as to folks around him But, as soon as that shut-up, solitary mind found anybody wanting it to do anything in confirmation of public opinion,—no! that mind would contract, as a snail in its spiral armor—and balk.

Lady Gadsby and His Honor, in talking about this, had thought of improving such a condition; but Simpkins was not a man to whom you could broach such a thought. It would only bring forth an outburst of sarcasm about "trying it on your own brain, first." So Branton Hills' Council always had so to word a "motion" as to, in a way, blind

Simpkins as to its import. Many such a motion had a hard fight showing him its valuation as a municipal law; such as our big Hall of Natural History, our Zoo, and so on.

Now nothing can so light up such a mind as a good laugh. Start a
man laughing, good, long and loud, and his mind's grimy windows will
slowly inch upward; snappy, invigorating air will rush in, and - lo! that
old snarling, ugly grouch will vanish as hoar-frost in a warm Spring
thaw!

And so it got around, on a bright Spring day, to Old Bill sitting on
Gadsby's front porch; outwardly calm, and smoking a good cigar
(which didn't blow up!), but, inwardly just full of snarls and growls
about Branton Hills' Youth.

"Silly half-grown young animals, found out that two plus two is four,
and thinking that *all* things will fit, just that way!"

Now that small girl, "of about six," who had had Nancy's baby out in
City Park, was passing Gadsby's mansion, and saw Old Bill. A kid of
six has, as you probably know, no formally laid-out plan for its daily
activity; anything bobbing up will attract. So, with this childish insta-
bility of thought, this tiny miss ran up onto Gadsby's porch and stood
in front of Old Bill, looking up at him, but saying not a word.

"Huh!" Bill just *had* to snort. "Looking at anything?"

"No, sir."

"What!! Oh, that is, you think 'not much,' probably. What do you
want, anyway.

"I want to play."

"All right; run along and play."

"No; I want to play with *you*."

"Pooh!! That's silly. I'm an old man. An old man can't play."

"Can, too. My Grandpa can."

"But I'm not your Grandpa, thank my lucky stars. Run along now;
I'm thinking."

"So am I."

"You? Huh! A kid can't think."

"Ooo-o! *I* can!"

"About what?"

"About playing with you."

Now Simpkins saw that this was a condition which wouldn't pass
with scowling or growling, but didn't know what to do about it. Play
with a kid? *What?* Councilman Simpkins pl—

But into that shut-up mind, through a parti*ally,—only* partially,—
rising window, was wafting a back thought of May Day in City Park;
and that happy, singing, marching ring of tots around that ribbon-
wound mast. Councilman Simpkins was in that ring.

So this thought got to tramping round and round many a musty corridor in his mind; throwing up a window, "busting in" a door, and shov-
ing a lot of dust and rubbish down a back stairway. Round and round it
ran, until, (!!) Old Bill, slowly and surprisingly softly, said:—

"What do you want to play?"

Oh! Oh! What a victory for that tot!! What a victory for *Youth!!* And
what a *fall* for grouchy, snarling Maturity!! I think that Simpkins, right
at that instant, *saw* that bright sunlight coming in through that rising
window; rising by baby hands; and from that "bust in" door. I think that
Old Bill cast off, in that instant, that hard, gloomy coating of dissatisfaction, which was gripping his shut-up mind. And I think,—in fact, I
know,—that Old Bill Simpkins was now,—that is, was—was—was, oh,
just plain *happy!*

"What do you want to play?"

"This is a lady, a-going to town."

"Play *what?*"

My!! Don't you know how to play that? All right; I'll show you.
Now just stick out your foot. That's it. Now I'll sit on it, so. Now you
bump it up and down. Ha, ha! Ho, ho! That's it! This is a lady, a-going
to town, a-going to town, a-going to town! And as that tiny lady sang
that baby song gaily and happily, Old Bill was actually laughing; and
laughing *uproariously,* too!

As this sight was occurring, His Honor and Lady Gadsby, looking out
from a parlor window, Gadsby said, happily:—

"A lady physician is working on Old Bill," causing Lady Gadsby to
add:

"And a mighty good doctor, too."

IT WAS NIGHT again.

That small Salvation Army group was parading and singing, A young
girl would soon start a long oration against drink. Now boys, gawking
as boys always do, saw a shadowy form of a man slinking along from
doorway to doorway, plainly watching this marching group, but also,
plainly trying to stay out of sight. A halt, a song or two, and Mary Antor was soon walking towards Old Lady Flanagan's cabin. But!! In

passing big, dark City Park, a man, rushing wildly up, wrapping that frail form in a cast-iron grip, planting kiss upon kiss upon Mary's lips, finally unwound that grip and stood stiffly in military saluting position. Mary, naturally in a bad fright, took a short, anxious, inquiring look, and instantly, all that part of City Park actually *rang* with a wild girlish cry:—

"Norman!!!"

"Hulloa, kiddo! Just got in, half an hour ago, on a small troop train; and, by luck, saw you marching in that group. *Wow!!* But you do look *grand!"*

"And you look grand, too, Norman; but—but—but—not drunk?"

"No, sis! Not for many a day now. Saw too much of it in camp. Big, grand, corking good chaps down and out from it. Days and days in jail, military jail, you know, and finally finding a 'bad conduct' stamp on Company books. No, sir; I'm off it, *for good!"*

~ ~ ~ ~ ~

ON OLD LADY Flanagan's porch Mary sat way past midnight with, no, not with Norman, only, but with *two* khaki-clad boys; and it was miraculous that that small, loving childish bosom could hold so much joy! Old Lady Flanagan in nightgown and cap, looking down a front stairway, (and Old Man Flanagan, also in nightgown and cap, and also looking down), said:—

"Arrah!! Go wan oop stairs, you snoopin' varmit!"

"Who's a snoopin' varmint? Not *you,* of –"

"Go wan oop, I say! By golly! That darlin' girl has found a mountain of gold wid Norman an' –"

"Who's that wid Norman? That guy's around, nights, now, as—"

"Say, you!! Do you go oop? Or do I swat you?"

BILL GADSBY, going abroad, naturally wasn't on that ballot for Councilman Antor's chair; but this history shows that that mouthy antagonist who had had so much to say about "pink satin ribbons" and "vanilla sprays, didn't win. No. A first class *man* got that position; old Tom Young, Sarah's Dad, as good an old soul as any in all Branton Hills. And was Sarah happy! Oh, my! And was Sarah proud! Two "oh mys!" Tiny Nancy, loyal as always to Bill, said:—

"Bill was as good as in, for nobody, knowing my Bill would ballot against him; and Bill would hold that honor now, but for 'Old Glory's' calling."

That's right, Nancy darling, you stick up for Bill; for, though Bill didn't know it until many months, a citation "for outstanding and valorous conduct in action" was soon to go through our National Printing Plant! For a "city fop" or an "outdoor part of a tailor shop" is not always a boob, you know.

Gadsby's mansion was again brightly aglow that night, that "World War flag" not hanging in his window now. And so, on Labor Day night, Lady Gadsby and His Honor, sitting in his parlor, thought that a light footfall was sounding out on his porch. As Gadsby got up to find out about it, Julius, coming in with a young girl, stood looking, grinningly, at Lady Gadsby; who, jumping up, said, happily:—

"Why! Mary Antor!"

"No, Ma," said Julius. "This is not Mary Antor."

"Not Mary Antor? Why, Julius, I think I know M—"

"Not Mary Antor, Ma, but Mary Gadsby!"

"Oh! Oh! My *darling* girl!!" and half crying and half laughing, Mary was snuggling in Lady Gadsby's arms; and His Honor, coming in, saying:—

"By golly! That young cuss, Cupid, is mighty busy around this town! Why, I can hardly walk two blocks along Broadway, without a young girl, who has 'grown up in a night,' stopping, and saying: 'Mayor Gadsby, this is my husband.' But I'll say that Cupid's marksmanship has always brought about happy matings. And, Mary, you darling kid, your sad, dark shadows will gradually pass; and Lady Gadsby and I will try to bring you loads and loads of comfort. But, say, you, Julius! I didn't know that you and Mary—"

"Ho, ho" said Mary, laughing. "Didn't you know that Julius and Norman and I sat out nights on old Lady Flanagan's porch?"

"Why, no; how should I? I don't go snooping around anybody's porch."

"Ha, ha, Dad," said Julius; "no snooping would find *that* out. Mary and I had had this plan so long ago that I didn't know a World War was coming!"

AS A SMALL boy, your historian was told that "A king was in his counting room, a-counting out his cash," or similar words, which told, practically, of his taking account of stock. So, also, Gadsby was on his thinking-porch, a-thinking of his past. (A mighty good thing to do, too; if anybody should ask you!)

"If," said His Honor, you can't find any fun during childhood, you naturally won't look for it as you grow up to maturity. You will grow 'hard,' and look upon fun as foolish. Also, if you don't furnish fun for a child, don't look for it to grow up bright, happy and loving. So, always put in a child's path an opportunity to watch, talk about, and know, as many good things as you can."

Lady Gadsby, from a parlor window, said:

"Practicing for a stumping tour, or a political pow-wow?"

"Ha, ha! No. Just thinking out loud."

So, as thinking cannot hurt anybody, His Honor was soon going on:—

"Affairs which look small or absurd to a full-grown man may loom up as big as a mountain to a child; and you shouldn't allow a fact that you saw a thing 'so much that I am sick of it,' to turn you away from an inquiring child. *You* wasn't sick of it, on that far-past day on which you first saw it. I always look back, happily and proudly, to taking a small girl to our City Florist's big glass building; to a group at our Night Court; a group finding out about dispatching our mail; and our circus! Boy! That *was* fun! Our awarding diplomas at City Hall; tiny Marian at our airport's inauguration; our Manual Training School graduation. *All* that did a big lot toward showing Youth that this big world is 'not half bad,' if adults will but watch, aid, and coach. And I *will not* stand anybody's snapping at a child! Particularly a tiny tot. If you think that you *must* snap, snap at a child so big as to snap back. I don't sanction 'talking back' to adults, but, ha, ha! I *did* find a grand, big *wallop* in Marian's April Fool cigar! Woo! *Did* Old Bill jump!! But that did no harm, and a sad young mind found a way to 'match things up with an antagonist. Now, just stand a child up against your body. How tall is it? Possibly only up to your hip. Still, a man,—or an animal *thinking* that it is a man—will slap, whip, or viciously *yank* an arm of so frail, so soft a tiny body! *That* is what *I* call a *coward!!* By golly! almost a *criminal!* If a tot is what you call naughty, (and no child voluntarily is,) why not lift that young body up onto your lap, and talk—don't *shout—about* what it just did? Shouting gains nothing with a tot. Man can shout at Man, at dogs, and at farm animals; but a man who shouts at a child is, at that instant, *sinking in his own muck of bullyism;* and bullyism is a sin, if anything in this world is. Ah *Youth!* You glorious dawn of Mankind! You bright, happy, glowing morning Sun; not at full brilliancy of noon, I know, but unavoidably on your way! *Youth!* How I do thrill at taking your warm, soft hand; walking with you; talking with you; but, most important of all, *laughing* with you! *That* is Man's pathway to glory. A man who drops blossoms in passing, will carry joy to folks along his way; a man who drops crumbs will also do a kindly act; but a man who drops kind words to a sobbing child will find his joy continuing for many a day; for blossoms will dry up; crumbs may blow away; but a kind word to a child may start a blossom growing in that young mind, which will so far surpass what an unkindly man might drop, as an orchid will surpass a wisp of grass. Just stop a bit and look back at your footprints along your past pathway. Did you put *many* humps in that soil which a small child might trip on? Did you angrily slam a door, which might so jolt a high-strung tot as to bring on nights and nights of insomnia? Did you so constantly snarl at it that it don't want you around? In fact, did you put any*thing* in that back-path of yours which could bring sorrow to a child? Or start its distrust of you, as its rightful *guardian?* If so, *go back* right now, man, and fix up such spots by kindly acts from now on. Or, *jump into a pond, and don't crawl out again!!* For nobody wants you around!"

Lady Gadsby, as this oration was wafting off amongst lilac shrubs, and across soft, warm lawns, had sat, also thinking; finally coming out onto that ivy-bound porch, and sitting down by His Honor, saying:—

"That was just grand, John, but I was thinking along a path varying a bit from that. You know that Man's brain is *actually* all of him. All parts of his body, as you follow down from his brain, act simply as aids to it. His nostrils bring him air; his mouth is for masticating his food; his hands and limbs furnish ability for manipulation and locomotion; and his lungs, stomach and all inward organs function *only* for that brain. If you look at a crowd you say that you saw lots of folks: but if you look at a man bathing in a pond; and if that man sank until only that part from his brow upward was in sight, you might say that you saw nobody; only a man's scalp. But you actually saw a man, for a man is only as big as that part still in sight. Now a child's skull, naturally, is not so big as a man's; so its brain has no room for all that vast mass of thoughts which adult brains contain. It is, so to say, in a small room. But, as days and months go by, that room will push its walls outward, and that young brain gradually fill up all that additional room. So, looking for calm, cool thinking in a child is as silly as looking for big, juicy plums amongst frail spring blossoms. Why, oh, *why* don't folks think of that? *You* know what foolish sounding things Julius was always asking, as a child. 'How can just rubbing a match light it?' 'Why is it dark at night?' 'Why can't a baby talk?' But, you and I, John, didn't laugh at him. No, not for an instant. And *now* look at our Julius and our Kathlyn; both famous, just through all that asking; and our aid. John, God *could* put Man into this world, full-grown. But God don't do so; for God knows that, without a tiny hand to hold, a tiny foot to pat, tiny lips to kiss, and a tiny, warm, wriggling body to hug, Man would know nothing but work."

Gadsby sat smoking for a bit, finally saying:—

"Darling, that pair of robins up in that big oak with four young, and you and I in this big building, also with four, know all about what you just said; and, and,—hmmm!! It's almost midnight." And His Honor's mansion was soon dark; bathing in soft moonlight.

PRACTICALLY ALL Branton Hills was talking about Councilman Simpkins; for Councilman Simpkins just didn't look natural; and Councilman Simpkins didn't act natural. In fact, Councilman Simpkins was crawling out of his old cocoon; and, though an ugly, snarling *dowdy* worm had lain for so long, shut up in that tight mass of wrappings around his brain, *now* a gay, smiling moth was coming out; for Councilman Simpkins was "dolling up!"

If Bill Gadsby was known as a "tailorshop's outdoor part," Old Bill was not a part. No, Old Bill *was* that tailor shop—outdoor, indoor, or without a door. In fact, Councilman Simpkins now had *"it,"* such as our films talk about so much today.

But Simpkins' outfit was not flashy or "loud." Suits of good cloth, hats of stylish form. always a bright carnation "just south of his chin," boots always glossy, and a smart, springy walk, had all Broadway gasping as this Apollo-vision swung jauntily along. Nancy, happy, giggling Nancy, was "all of a grin" about this magic trans formation; and, with that old, inborn instinct of womanhood, told Lucy:—

"You just watch, and mark my word. A woman is in this pudding! Old Bill just couldn't boom out in such a way without having a goal in sight; and I'll put up a dollar on it."

And Lucy, also a woman, said smilingly:—

"And I'll put up a dollar and a half!"

But His Honor and Lady Gadsby, at such talk would look skyward, cough, and say:—

"Possibly a woman; and a mighty young woman, at that."

Now, if anything will "warm up" a public, it is gossip; particularly if it is about mystifying actions of a public man; and this had soon grown to a point at which a particularly curious man or woman thought of going to Old Bill and boldly asking: "Who is it?" But, as I said, what Councilman Simpkins would say to such "butting in" was known to all Branton Hills. No. Councilman Simpkins could doll up and trot around all that that portly Solon might wish; but, so to say, a sign was always hanging from his coat front, saying:—

"HANDS OFF!!!"

~ ~ ~ ~ ~

NINA ADAMS and Virginia sat on Gadsby's porch with Nancy and Kathlyn; and Old Bill was up as a topic. Virginia, constantly smiling and inwardly chuckling, hadn't much to say about our frisky Councilman; and Nancy and Kathlyn couldn't fathom why. But Nina, not so backward, said:

"Pffft! If a man wants to throw old clothing away and buy stylish outfits, what affair is it, but his own? It isn't right so to pick out a man, and turn him into a laughing stock of a city. Old Bill isn't a bad sort; possibly born grouchy; but if a grouchy man or woman, (and I know a *bunch* of that class in this town!) *can* pull out of it, and laugh, and find a bit of joy in living, *I* think it is an occasion for congratulations, *not* booing."

"Oh," said Kathlyn, "I don't think anybody is booing Councilman Simpkins. But you know that any showing of such an innovation is apt to start gossip. Just why, I don't know. It, though, is a trait of Mankind only. Animals don't 'bloom' out so abruptly. You can hunt through Biology, Zoology or any similar study, and find but slow,—awfully slow,—adaptations toward any form of variation. Hurrying was not known until Man got around."

"My!" said Nancy, gasping, and not giggling now, "I wish that *I* could know all that you know, Kathy. As our slang puts it, 'I don't know nothin'.' "

"But, you could," said Kathlyn, "if you would only study. All through our young days, you know, with you and Bill out at a card or dancing party, you in flimsy frills, and Bill swishing around in sartorial glory, *I* was upstairs, studying. And so was Julius."

"That's right," said Nina. "I wish Virginia would study."

"Oh, I *am!*" said Virginia, all aglow. "You? Studying *what?*"

"Aviation! Harold is going to show—"

"Now, Virginia, Harold is *not!*" and Nina Adams' foot was *down!* "It's not so bad for a man to fly, but a girl—"

"But, Mama, lots of girls fly, nowadays."

"I know that, *and* I also know a girl who *won't!* And, just as Lucy has always known that Old Tom Young's 'no' *was* a no, just so had Nina Adams brought up Virginia.

"But," said Kathlyn, "this sky-shooting talk isn't finding out anything about Councilman Simpkins;" and Virginia said:—

"Possibly Old Bill wants to 'fly high.' I think I'll ask Harold about taking him up for a jaunt."

This, bringing a happy laugh all around, Nina said:—

"Now don't jolly poor Bill too much. I don't know what, or who, got him to 'going social.' " And Nancy, giggling, said:—

"I put up a dollar, with Lucy's dollar-fifty that it's a woman."

"Oh, I don't know, now," said Nina. "A man isn't always trotting around on a woman's apron strings," and, as it was growing dark, Nina and Virginia got up to go.

Passing down Gadsby's front walk, a soft night wind brought back to that porch:—

"Now, Virginia, quit this! You will stay *on solid ground!*"

"Aw, Ma! Harold says—"

But a big bus, roaring by, cut it short.

~ ~ ~ ~ ~

JUST A MONTH from this, His Honor, sitting on his porch with his "Morning Post" ran across a short bit, just two rows of print, which had him calling "Hi!" which Lady Gadsby took as a signal for a quick trip to that porch.

"All right, Your Honor! On duty! What's up?"

Gadsby, folding his "Post" into a narrow column, and handing it to that waiting lady, said nothing. As that good woman saw that paragraph. Gadsby saw first a gasp, following that, a grin, and finally:—

"Why! Of all things! So *that's* Nina—"

That row of print said, simply:—

"By Pastor Brown, on Saturday night, in Pastor's study, Nina Adams and Councilman Simpkins."

"Why!" said Lady Gadsby, laughing, "Nina sat on this porch only last month, talking about Old Bill, but saying nothing about this! I'm going right around to hug that darling woman; for *that* is what I call *tact.*"

So, as Nina and our Lady sat talking, Nina said:

"*You* know that Bill and I, growing up from kids in school, always got along grandly; no childhood spats; but, still it was no 'crush' such as Youth falls into. As Bill got out of high school, I still had two rooms to go through. You also know that I wasn't a 'Miss' for long from graduation day. But Irving Adams was lost in that awful 'Titanic' calamity, and I brought up my baby in my widowhood. Bill was always sympathizing and patronizing, though all Branton Hills thought him a cast-iron grouch. But a public man is not always stiff and hard in his off hours; and Bill and I, slowly but gradually finding many a happy hour could—

"All right, you grand, luscious thing!!" and Lady Gadsby and Nina sat laughing on a couch, as in old, old school days. "And," said Nina, happily; "poor Bill's upstairs, now, putting his things around to suit him. Living for so long in a small lodging all his things staid in a trunk. A lodging-room always has various folks around, you know, and a man don't lay his things out as in his *own* room. So—"

"Nina," said Lady Gadsby; "do you know what brought him out of his old shut-in way of looking at things?"

"From just a word or two Bill drops, occasionally, I think that a child is—"

And Lady Gadsby, said; "You know our Good Book's saying about: 'And a tiny child shall—' "

SIX MONTHS from that day upon which old Mars, God of War had angrily thrown down his cannons, tanks, gas-bombs and so on, fuming at Man's inability to "stand up to it, Gadsby's mansion was dark again. Not totally dark; just his parlor lamp, and a light or two in halls and on stairways. And so this history found Nancy and Kathlyn out on that moon-lit porch; Nancy sobbing, fighting it off, and sobbing again. Tall, studious, loving Kathlyn, sitting fondly by Nancy's tiny form, said;—

"Now, sis; I wouldn't cry so much, for I don't think that conditions, just now, call for it."

"B-b-b-but I'd stop if I could, wouldn't I?" and poor Nancy was sobbing again. *"Now, wait!"* and Kathlyn, uncommonly cross, vigorously shook Nancy's arm. *"You* can't gain a *thing* this way. Mama is probably all right. Oh, is that you, Daddy?"

His Honor sat down by his two girls. Gadsby was not looking good. Black rings around his always laughing orbs; a hard cast to that jovial mouth; a gray hair or two, cropping up amongst his wavy brown. But Gadsby was not old. Oh, no; far from it. Still, that stoop in walking; that odd, limp slump in sitting; that toning down in joviality, had, for six months past, had all Branton Hills sympathizing with its popular Mayor.

~ ~ ~ ~ ~

DAYS; DAYS; DAYS! And, oh! that *tough* part,—nights, nights, nights! Nights of two young chaps, in full clothing, only just napping on a parlor conch. Nights of two girls nodding in chairs in a dimly,— oh, *so* dimly a lit room.

It got around almost to Christmas, only a fortnight to that happy day; but,—happy in Gadsby's mansion? Finally Frank took a hand:—"Now, kid, *do* try to stop this crying! You know I'm not scolding you, darling, but, you *just can't* go on, this way; and *that's that!"*

"I'm trying *so* hard, hubby!"

Now Nancy was of that good, sturdy old Colonial stock of His Honor and Lady Gadsby; and so, as Christmas was approaching, and many a bunch of holly hung in Broadway's big windows, and as many a Salvation Army Santa Claus stood at its curbs, Nancy's constitution won out; but a badly worn young lady was in and out of Gadsby's mansion daily; bringing baby Lillian to kiss Grandma, and riding back with Frank at about six o'clock.

~ ~ ~ ~ ~

OLD DOCTOR Wilkins, coming in on a cool. sharp night, found His Honor, Nancy, Kathlyn, Bill, Julius, Lucy, Mary, Frank and John all in that big parlor.

"Now, you bunch, it's up to you. Lady Gadsby will pull through all right," (Nancy rushing wildly to kiss him!) "it hangs now upon good nursing; and I know you will furnish that. And I will say without a wisp of a doubt, that a calm, happy room; not too many around; and—and—hmmm!! Julius, can't you hunt around in our woods that you and Kathlyn know so thoroughly, and find a tall, straight young fir; cut it down, rig it up with lights and a lot of shiny stuff; stand it up in your Ma's room, and—"

~ ~ ~ ~ ~

'Tis a night, almost Christmas,
And all through that room
A warm joy is stirring;
No sign of a gloom.
And "Ma," sitting up,
In gay gown, and cap,
No, no! *Will not* start
On a long wintry nap!
For, out on that lawn
A group of girls stand;
A group singing carols
With part of our Band.
And that moon, in full vigor,
Was lustrous; and lo!
Our Lady is singing!
Aha, *now* I know
That Nancy and Kathlyn
And Julius and Bill
And also His Honor,
Will sing with a will!
And Old Doctor Wilkins
Amidst it all stands;
Smiting and nodding,
And rubbing his hands;
And, sliding out, slyly;
Calls back at that sight:—
"Happy Christmas to all;
And to all a Good Night!"

ALONG ABOUT midnight a happy group sat around Gadsby's parlor lamp, as Dr. Wilkins was saying:—

"Stopping a war; that is, stopping actual military combat, is not stopping a war in *all* its factors. During continuous hard strain a human mind can hold up; and it is truly amazing how much it can stand. Day by day, with that war-strain of worry pulling it down, it staunchly holds aloof, as a mighty oak in facing a storm. But it has a limit!! With too much and too long strain, it will *snap;* just as that mighty oak will fall, in a long fight. Lady Gadsby will avoid such a snap though it is by a narrow margin."

As this group sat in that holly-hung parlor, with that big cloth sign in big gold capitals; HAPPY CHRISTMAS, across its back wall; with horns tooting outdoors; with many a window around town aglow with tiny, dancing tallow-dip lights; with baby Lillian "all snuggling—so warm in a cot; as vision of sugar plums"—(and why *shouldn't* a baby think of sugar plums on that night, almost Christmas?); as, I say, this happy group sat around Gadsby's lamp, Mars, that grim old war tyrant, was far, far away. Upstairs, calmly snoozing on a big downy pillow, Lady Gadsby was now rapidly coming back again to that buxom, happy-go-lucky First Lady of Branton Hills.

CHRISTMAS, GAY and happy in Gadsby's mansion, was soon far, far back. A robin or two was hopping about on His Honor's lawn, looking for a squirming lunch; Lady was taking short walks with Nancy; Kathlyn having to go back to work in our big hospital. Lilac, syringa, narcissus, tulips, hyacinths burst out in a riot of bloom; and a bright warm Sun brought joy to all. And so this history found His Honor on his porch with his "Post" as a young lad, coming up, said;—"Good morning, sir. I'm soliciting funds for a big stadium for Branton Hills, which will furnish an opportunity for football, polo,—"

"Whoa!" said Gadsby, putting down his "Post" and looking critically at his young visitor. "You look a bit familiar, boy. Oho! If is isn't kid Banks; oh, pardon!—*Allan* Banks; son of Councilman Banks! You young folks grow up so fast I don't know half of you. Now what about this soliciting. Who is back of you?"

"Branton Hills' Organization of Youth; Part Two, sir."

"Branton Hills Org—Ha, ha! Upon my word! Who is starting this group?"

Mary, coming out from His Honor's parlor, said:—

"Oh, I forgot to notify you of this. Norman has got about fifty kids from Grammar School boys and girls, anxious to follow in *your* Organization's foot-prints."

Was Gadsby happy? Did Gadsby thrill? Did that long-past, happy day float in glowing colors through his mind? It did. And now that old, hard-working bunch of kids, grown up, now, and with kids of its own; that loyal bunch of young sprouts was taking root; was born again!

Oh, *how* Youth crawls tip on you! Flow a tiny girl "almost instantly" shoots up into a tall, charming young woman! *How* a top-spinning, ball-tossing, racing, shouting boy looms up into a manly young chap in Military School uniform! Gadsby *was* happy; for, wasn't this a tonic for his spinal column? So His Honor said;—

"Allan, I think Branton Hills will officially aid this stadium plan. I'll put it up to Council." But, Allan Banks, *not* Kid Banks now, was just so old as to know a thing or two about Council bills; and, out as a solicitor, naturally sought a good showing on donations won, so said;—

"A Council donation will fit in grand, sir; but how about grouchy old Bill Simpk—"

"Trot along, Allan."

"But how about this stadium? I'm doubting Old B—"

"Trot along, Allan."

~ ~ ~ ~ ~

WHAT MARY HAD said was a fact. Norman Antor had not only fought a military war; Norman Antor had also fought an *inward* war. A war, which fought him with gallon jugs, small phials, spoons, mixing apparatus, and—a stumbling, mumbling *stupor!* Norman had fought with about two million lads in that military war; but now, with no aid but a strain of good blood, starting way back of his carousing Dad (but, as such traits may, skipping a notch or two, and implanting in this young lad just a grain of its old nobility of mind), was fighting again; and, just as any solitary young chap amongst that two million loyally did his part, just so was this tiny grain now doing *its* part; fighting valiantly in his brain. It was giving him torturing thoughts in army night-camps, of a darling, loving young girl, a part of his own family, growing up "in a pool of liquor;" thoughts in night-camps of Branton Hills' patrol-wagon trips to jail; and *Darn* that thought of Virginia! Virginia *drunk* by his own hand! Ugh!! *Why not chop that stinking hand off?* And, on coming back to Branton Hills, watching that darling Mary in Salvation Army uniform, tramping, talking, praying for just such low-down "liquor hounds" as—.

Oh! It was an awful fight! A long, brain-racking onslaught against a villain shut in by walls of iron! But though Norman Antor's night— camp fights with Norman Antor had "put a big kick" in his wish to "lay off that stuff," just a final blow, just an awful brain-crashing *blast* was still missing, so that that big right hand might point skyward, to clinch that vow. And that blast was waiting for Norman! To anybody standing around, it wasn't much of a blast; but it *was!* It was a mighty concussion of T.N.T., coming as Mary, young, loving, praying Mary, said, as his arms unwound from around that frail form;—

"Why, Norman! *Not drunk?"*

God!! What flashing, shooting, sizzling sparks shot through his brain!! Up, out, in; all kinds of ways!! *What* crashing bombs!!

And, that first calm night on Old Lady Flanagan's porch; that moonlit night of bliss, with soft, cuddling, snuggling, laughing, crying darling Mary!

"I say," Norman was shouting, inwardly; "that night of bliss *was a* night of bliss and *don't anybody try to say that it wasn't!"*

For it was a night on which a young man's Soul *was back;* hack in its own Mind, now full of God's incomparably grand *purity!*

~ ~ ~ ~ ~

LADY GADSBY was visiting Nina, sitting in that big front parlor; Virginia sitting calmly rocking; (and, hmmm! That was about all Virginia *ought* to do, just now!) A young High School girl, coming in, said:—"Good morning! I'm soliciting for funds for a stadium for –"

"Marian!" sang out Virginia, *"What's* all this? *You* soliciting?"

"Why not?" said Marian, brightly. "Norman Antor's Organization of Youth; Part Two, is soli—"

"Norman Antor's *what?* and Virginia was all agog in an instant, as Marian Hopkins told all about it; and, with childish flippancy, forgot all about soliciting, saying:—

"I was told that Harold is giving flying instructions. Don't you want to fly? My! *I do!"*

"I *did,"* said Virginia, softly; "but,—not now; and Marian was a bit too young to know why Lady Gadsby was smiling at Nina!

As Nancy found out about this, on Lady Gadsby's coming back to lunch, that "old Branton Hills matron," as Gadsby found a lot of fun calling "his baby girl," now-a-days, said, giggling:—

"No! Virginia! You'll *stay on solid ground!*"

LADY GADSBY and His Honor sat in Branton Hills' First Church, on a hot July Sunday. Out-doors, twitting birds, lacy clouds, and gay blossoms, told of happy hours in this long, bright month. Pastor Brown, announcing a hymn, said:—

"This is a charming hymn. Our choir always sings it without company; but today, I want *all* you good folks to join in. Just pour forth your joy and sing it, good and strongly."

That hymn had six stanzas; and Gadsby, noting an actually *grand* bass singing just back of him, thought of turning around, from curiosity; and as that fifth stanza was starting, said to Lady Gadsby:—

"Do you know who that is, singing that grand bass part?"

Lady Gadsby didn't; but Lady Gadsby was a woman; and, from Noah's Ark to Branton Hills' First Church, woman, as a branch of Mankind, was curious. So a slow casual turning brought a dig in His honor's ribs:—"it's Norman Antor!"

Pastor Brown, standing at that big church door as folks, filing out would stop for a word or two, said to Gadsby:—

"Young Antor is invariably in church, now-a-days. I may add to my choir, and am thinking of putting him in it. I'm so glad to find out about that boy winning his fight. I always *thought* Norman would turn out all right."

Pastor Brown was right; and two Branton Hills girls, a Salvation Army lady, and a tiny tot of six had won crowns of Glory, from throwing rays of light into two badly stagnant Minds.

THIRTY-SIX MONTHS. That's not so long a run in daily affairs, and this Branton Hills history finds Thanksgiving Day dawning. In Branton Hill's locality it is not, customarily, what you would call a cold day. Many a Thanksgiving has had warm, balmy air, and without snow; though, also, without all that vast army of tiny chirping, singing, buzzing things on lawn or branch. But contrast has its own valuation; for, through it, common sights, vanishing annually, show up *with a* happy joy, upon coming back. Ah! That first faint coloring of grass, in Spring!

That baby bud, on shrub or plant, shyly asking our loving South Wind if it's all right to pop out, now. That sprouting of big brown limbs on oak and birch; that first "blush of Spring" in orchards; that first furry, fuzzy, cuddly spray of pussy willows! Spring and Fall; two big points in your trip along your Pathway. Fall with its rubbish from months of labor corn-stalks, brown, dry grass, old twigs lying around, wilting plants; bright colorings blazing in distant woodlands; chill winds crawling in through windows, at night. And Spring! Pick-up, paint-up, wash-up Spring!! So, as I said, Branton Hills got around to Thanksgiving Day; that day on which as many of a family as possibly can should sit around a common board; coming from afar, or from only a door or two away.

Gadsby's dining-room was not big; it had always sat but six in his family. But, on *this* Thanksgiving Day,—hmmm! "Wait, now—uh-huh, that's it. Just run that pair of sliding doors back, put that parlor lamp upstairs; and that piano? Why not roll it out into my front hall? I know it will look odd, but you can't go through a Thanksgiving soup to nuts' standing up. *Got* to jam in chairs, any old way!"

But who is all this mob that will turn His Honor's dining-room into a thirty-foot hail? I'll look around, as our happy, laughing, singing, clapping group sits down to Gadsby's Thanksgiving party.

I find *two* "posts of honor;" (My gracious! *so* far apart!); His Honor, with carving tools filling dish, dish, and dish.

"Atta boy! Atta girl! Pass up your chow-dish! This bird has but two drum-sticks, but six of his cousins wait, out in our cook-shop! Lots of grub! What's that, Julius? A bit of dark? Want any gravy?"

At Post Two sits "Ma;" again in that good old buxom condition, so familiar to all Branton Hills;—

"Right this way, folks, for potato, squash, onions, carrots and turnip!!"

What a happy bunch! Following around from Gadsby, sit Bill, Lucy and Addison. But whoa! Who's this Addison? Oh, pardon; I forgot all about it. Lucy's baby; and his first Thanksgiving. Hi, you! Tut-tut! Mustn't grab raisins! Naughty, naughty! On Lucy's right sit Mary, Julius and Norman; following along, I find Nancy, Frank and Baby Lillian, Kathlyn, John, Lady Standish, Priscilla and Hubby Arthur Rankin; Nina Adams,—Oh! A *thousand* pardons!!—Nina *Simpkins!* and Old Bill. Say! You wouldn't know Bill! Bright, happy, laughing, singing, and tapping a cup with his spoon; spick-span suit, and that now

121

famous "Broadway carnation." Hulloa, Bill; you old sport!! Glad to find you looking so happy! What? *Two* whacks at that bird? Why Bill!! On Bill's right sits Pastor Brown, old Doctor Wilkins, Harold, Virginia, and Patricia. Oh, pardon again! Patricia, Virginia's baby; just six months old, today, and valiantly trying to swallow a half-pound candy cow! Following around I find Old Tom Young, Sarah, and Paul. No, I don't find a high-chair by Sarah; but Sarah sits just rocking, rocking, rocking, now-a-days. Following on, again, is Old Tom Donaldson, Clancy Dowd, and—Old Lady Flanagan, with "this dom thing I calls hoosband!" And lastly, Marian and old Pat Ryan from our railway station's trunk room.

So it was just laugh, talk, "stuff," and—

~ ~ ~ ~ ~

OH, HUM! Folks can't stay all night, you know; so, finally, groups and pairs, drifting out, all had happy words for His Honor and Lady Gadsby; and His Honor, a word or two; for you know Gadsby *can* talk? So it was:—

"Good night, Nina; good luck, Old Bill! Oh! say, Bill; will *that* cigar blow up? Good night, Virginia; and ta-ta Patricia; and Virginia, you mind your Ma and stay down on solid ground! Aha, Clancy! You old motor-pump fan! No; that's wrong; *animal-drawn* pump! Good night, Pastor Brown; so glad you put Norman in your choir. And now Old Tom and Sarah! Tom, you look as young as on that day on which you brought Sarah, just a tiny, squalling, fist-waving bunch, to this porch to ask about adoption! And I know Sarah has always had a kind, loving Dad. Paul, you young sprout! As *you* turn into a daddy, soon now, you'll find that, on marrying, a man and woman start actually living. It's miraculous, Paul, that's just what it is."

And so it was; pairs and groups shaking hands and laughing, until finally a big buxom woman sang out:—

"Whoops!! It was a *wow* of a grub-lay-out! It *was* thot! But this dom thing I calls hoosband. Say! You grub-stuffin' varmint! Phwat's that in your hat? A droom-stick, is it? Do you want His Honor to think I don't cook nuthin' for you? Goodnight, all! I'm thot full I'm almost a-bustin'!"

As Lady Standish shook hands, that worthy woman said:—

"John, what you did for Branton Hills should go into our National

Library at Washington, in plain sight."

"Sally, *Youth's* part was paramount in all that work. All I did was to boss;" and Old Doc Wilkins, coming out, nibbling a bunch of raisins, said:—

"Uh-huh; but a boss must know his job!"

"That's all right," said Gadsby; "but it was *young hands and young minds* that did my work! Don't disqualify Youth for it will fool you, if you do!"

~ ~ ~ ~ ~

A GLORIOUS FULL moon sails across a sky without a cloud. A crisp night air has folks turning up coat collars and kids hopping up and down for warmth. And that giant star, Sirius, winking slyly, knows that soon, now, that light up in His Honor's room window will go out. Fttt! It *is* out! So, as Sirius and Luna hold an all-night vigil, I'll say a soft "Good-night" to all our happy bunch, and to John Gadsby—Youth's Champion.

FINIS

RAMBLE HOUSE's

HARRY STEPHEN KEELER WEBWORK MYSTERIES

(RH) indicates the title is available ONLY in the **RAMBLE HOUSE** edition

The Ace of Spades Murder
The Affair of the Bottled Deuce (RH)
The Amazing Web
The Barking Clock
Behind That Mask
The Book with the Orange Leaves
The Bottle with the Green Wax Seal
The Box from Japan
The Case of the Canny Killer
The Case of the Crazy Corpse (RH)
The Case of the Flying Hands (RH)
The Case of the Ivory Arrow
The Case of the Jeweled Ragpicker
The Case of the Lavender Gripsack
The Case of the Mysterious Moll
The Case of the 16 Beans
The Case of the Transparent Nude (RH)
The Case of the Transposed Legs
The Case of the Two-Headed Idiot (RH)
The Case of the Two Strange Ladies
The Circus Stealers (RH)
Cleopatra's Tears
A Copy of Beowulf (RH)
The Crimson Cube (RH)
The Face of the Man From Saturn
Find the Clock
The Five Silver Buddhas
The 4th King
The Gallows Waits, My Lord! (RH)
The Green Jade Hand
Finger! Finger!
Hangman's Nights (RH)
I, Chameleon (RH)
I Killed Lincoln at 10:13! (RH)
The Iron Ring
The Man Who Changed His Skin (RH)
The Man with the Crimson Box
The Man with the Magic Eardrums
The Man with the Wooden Spectacles
The Marceau Case
The Matilda Hunter Murder
The Monocled Monster

The Murder of London Lew
The Murdered Mathematician
The Mysterious Card (RH)
The Mysterious Ivory Ball of Wong Shing Li (RH)
The Mystery of the Fiddling Cracksman
The Peacock Fan
The Photo of Lady X (RH)
The Portrait of Jirjohn Cobb
Report on Vanessa Hewstone (RH)
Riddle of the Travelling Skull
Riddle of the Wooden Parrakeet (RH)
The Scarlet Mummy (RH)
The Search for X-Y-Z
The Sharkskin Book
Sing Sing Nights
The Six From Nowhere (RH)
The Skull of the Waltzing Clown
The Spectacles of Mr. Cagliostro
Stand By—London Calling!
The Steeltown Strangler
The Stolen Gravestone (RH)
Strange Journey (RH)
The Strange Will
The Straw Hat Murders (RH)
The Street of 1000 Eyes (RH)
Thieves' Nights
Three Novellos (RH)
The Tiger Snake
The Trap (RH)
Vagabond Nights (Defrauded Yeggman)
Vagabond Nights 2 (10 Hours)
The Vanishing Gold Truck
The Voice of the Seven Sparrows
The Washington Square Enigma
When Thief Meets Thief
The White Circle (RH)
The Wonderful Scheme of Mr. Christopher Thorne
X. Jones—of Scotland Yard
Y. Cheung, Business Detective

Keeler Related Works

A To Izzard: A Harry Stephen Keeler Companion by Fender Tucker — Articles and stories about Harry, by Harry, and in his style. Included is a compleat bibliography.

Wild About Harry: Reviews of Keeler Novels — Edited by Richard Polt & Fender Tucker — 22 reviews of works by Harry Stephen Keeler from *Keeler News*. A perfect introduction to the author.

The Keeler Keyhole Collection: Annotated newsletter rants from Harry Stephen Keeler, edited by Francis M. Nevins. Over 400 pages of incredibly personal Keeleriana.

Fakealoo — Pastiches of the style of Harry Stephen Keeler by selected demented members of the HSK Society. Updated every year with the new winner.

RAMBLE HOUSE's OTHER LOONS

Strands of the Web: Short Stories of Harry Stephen Keeler — Edited and Introduced by Fred Cleaver
The Sam McCain Novels — Ed Gorman's terrific series includes *The Day the Music Died, Wake Up Little Susie* and *Will You Still Love Me Tomorrow?*
A Shot Rang Out — Three decades of reviews from Jon Breen
Blood Moon — The first of the Robert Payne series by Ed Gorman
The Time Armada — Fox B. Holden's 1953 SF gem.
Black River Falls — Suspense from the master, Ed Gorman
Sideslip — 1968 SF masterpiece by Ted White and Dave Van Arnam
The Triune Man — Mindscrambling science fiction from Richard A. Lupoff
Detective Duff Unravels It — Episodic mysteries by Harvey O'Higgins
Mysterious Martin, the Master of Murder — Two versions of a strange 1912 novel by Tod Robbins about a man who writes books that can kill.
The Master of Mysteries — 1912 novel of supernatural sleuthing by Gelett Burgess
Dago Red — 22 tales of dark suspense by Bill Pronzini
The Night Remembers — A 1991 Jack Walsh mystery from Ed Gorman
Rough Cut & New, Improved Murder — Ed Gorman's first two novels
Hollywood Dreams — A novel of the Depression by Richard O'Brien
Six Gelett Burgess Novels — *The Master of Mysteries, The White Cat, Two O'Clock Courage, Ladies in Boxes, Find the Woman, The Heart Line*
The Organ Reader — A huge compilation of just about everything published in the 1971-1972 radical bay-area newspaper, *THE ORGAN*.
A Clear Path to Cross — Sharon Knowles short mystery stories by Ed Lynskey
Old Times' Sake — Short stories by James Reasoner from Mike Shayne Magazine
Freaks and Fantasies — Eerie tales by Tod Robbins, collaborator of Tod Browning on the film FREAKS.
Five Jim Harmon Sleaze Double Novels — *Vixen Hollow/Celluloid Scandal, The Man Who Made Maniacs/Silent Siren, Ape Rape/Wanton Witch, Sex Burns Like Fire/Twist Session,* and *Sudden Lust/Passion Strip.* More doubles to come!
Marblehead: A Novel of H.P. Lovecraft — A long-lost masterpiece from Richard A. Lupoff. Published for the first time!
The Compleat Ova Hamlet — Parodies of SF authors by Richard A. Lupoff – New edition!
The Secret Adventures of Sherlock Holmes — Three Sherlockian pastiches by the Brooklyn author/publisher, Gary Lovisi.
The Universal Holmes — Richard A. Lupoff's 2007 collection of five Holmesian pastiches and a recipe for giant rat stew.
Four Joel Townsley Rogers Novels — By the author of *The Red Right Hand: Once In a Red Moon, Lady With the Dice, The Stopped Clock, Never Leave My Bed*
Two Joel Townsley Rogers Story Collections — Night of Horror and Killing Time
Twenty Norman Berrow Novels — *The Bishop's Sword, Ghost House, Don't Go Out After Dark, Claws of the Cougar, The Smokers of Hashish, The Secret Dancer, Don't Jump Mr. Boland!, The Footprints of Satan, Fingers for Ransom, The Three Tiers of Fantasy, The Spaniard's Thumb, The Eleventh Plague, Words Have Wings, One Thrilling Night, The Lady's in Danger, It Howls at Night, The Terror in the Fog, Oil Under the Window, Murder in the Melody, The Singing Room*
The N. R. De Mexico Novels — Robert Bragg presents *Marijuana Girl, Madman on a Drum, Private Chauffeur* in one volume.
Four Chelsea Quinn Yarbro Novels featuring Charlie Moon — *Ogilvie, Tallant and Moon, Music When the Sweet Voice Dies, Poisonous Fruit* and *Dead Mice*
Four Walter S. Masterman Mysteries — *The Green Toad, The Flying Beast, The Yellow Mistletoe* and *The Wrong Verdict,* fantastic impossible plots. More to come.
Two Hake Talbot Novels — *Rim of the Pit, The Hangman's Handyman.* Classic locked room mysteries.
Two Alexander Laing Novels — *The Motives of Nicholas Holtz* and *Dr. Scarlett,* stories of medical mayhem and intrigue from the 30s.
Four David Hume Novels — *Corpses Never Argue, Cemetery First Stop, Make Way for the Mourners, Eternity Here I Come,* and more to come.
Three Wade Wright Novels — *Echo of Fear, Death At Nostalgia Street* and *It Leads to Murder,* with more to come!
Five Rupert Penny Novels — *Policeman's Holiday, Policeman's Evidence, Lucky Policeman, Sealed Room Murder* and *Sweet Poison,* classic impossible mysteries.

126

Five Jack Mann Novels — Strange murder in the English countryside. *Gees' First Case, Nightmare Farm, Grey Shapes, The Ninth Life, The Glass Too Many.*

Seven Max Afford Novels — *Owl of Darkness, Death's Mannikins, Blood on His Hands, The Dead Are Blind, The Sheep and the Wolves, Sinners in Paradise* and *Two Locked Room Mysteries and a Ripping Yarn* by one of Australia's finest novelists.

Five Joseph Shallit Novels — *The Case of the Billion Dollar Body, Lady Don't Die on My Doorstep, Kiss the Killer, Yell Bloody Murder, Take Your Last Look.* One of America's best 50's authors.

Two Crimson Clown Novels — By Johnston McCulley, author of the Zorro novels, *The Crimson Clown* and *The Crimson Clown Again.*

The Best of 10-Story Book — edited by Chris Mikul, over 35 stories from the literary magazine Harry Stephen Keeler edited.

A Young Man's Heart — A forgotten early classic by Cornell Woolrich

The Anthony Boucher Chronicles — edited by Francis M. Nevins
Book reviews by Anthony Boucher written for the *San Francisco Chronicle*, 1942 – 1947. Essential and fascinating reading.

Muddled Mind: Complete Works of Ed Wood, Jr. — David Hayes and Hayden Davis deconstruct the life and works of a mad genius.

Gadsby — A lipogram (a novel without the letter E). Ernest Vincent Wright's last work, published in 1939 right before his death.

My First Time: The One Experience You Never Forget — Michael Birchwood — 64 true first-person narratives of how they lost it.

Automaton — Brilliant treatise on robotics: 1928-style! By H. Stafford Hatfield

The Incredible Adventures of Rowland Hern — Rousing 1928 impossible crimes by Nicholas Olde.

Slammer Days — Two full-length prison memoirs: *Men into Beasts* (1952) by George Sylvester Viereck and *Home Away From Home* (1962) by Jack Woodford

Murder in Black and White — 1931 classic tennis whodunit by Evelyn Elder

Killer's Caress — Cary Moran's 1936 hardboiled thriller

The Golden Dagger — 1951 Scotland Yard yarn by E. R. Punshon

Beat Books #1 — Two beatnik classics, *A Sea of Thighs* by Ray Kainen and *Village Hipster* by J.X. Williams

A Smell of Smoke — 1951 English countryside thriller by Miles Burton

Ruled By Radio — 1925 futuristic novel by Robert L. Hadfield & Frank E. Farncombe

Murder in Silk — A 1937 Yellow Peril novel of the silk trade by Ralph Trevor

The Case of the Withered Hand — 1936 potboiler by John G. Brandon

Finger-prints Never Lie — A 1939 classic detective novel by John G. Brandon

Inclination to Murder — 1966 thriller by New Zealand's Harriet Hunter

Invaders from the Dark — Classic werewolf tale from Greye La Spina

Fatal Accident — Murder by automobile, a 1936 mystery by Cecil M. Wills

The Devil Drives — A prison and lost treasure novel by Virgil Markham

Dr. Odin — Douglas Newton's 1933 potboiler comes back to life.

The Chinese Jar Mystery — Murder in the manor by John Stephen Strange, 1934

The Julius Caesar Murder Case — A classic 1935 re-telling of the assassination by Wallace Irwin that's much more fun than the Shakespeare version

West Texas War and Other Western Stories — by Gary Lovisi

The Contested Earth and Other SF Stories — A never-before published space opera and seven short stories by Jim Harmon.

Tales of the Macabre and Ordinary — Modern twisted horror by Chris Mikul, author of the *Bizarrism* series.

The Gold Star Line — Seaboard adventure from L.T. Reade and Robert Eustace.

The Werewolf vs the Vampire Woman — Hard to believe ultraviolence by either Arthur M. Scarm or Arthur M. Scram.

Black Hogan Strikes Again — Australia's Peter Renwick pens a tale of the outback.

Don Diablo: Book of a Lost Film — Two-volume treatment of a western by Paul Landres, with diagrams. Intro by Francis M. Nevins.

The Charlie Chaplin Murder Mystery — Movie hijinks by Wes D. Gehring

The Koky Comics — A collection of all of the 1978-1981 Sunday and daily comic strips by Richard O'Brien and Mort Gerberg, in two volumes.

Suzy — Another collection of comic strips from Richard O'Brien and Bob Vojtko

Dime Novels: Ramble House's 10-Cent Books — *Knife in the Dark* by Robert Leslie Bellem, *Hot Lead* and *Song of Death* by Ed Earl Repp, *A Hashish House in New York* by H.H. Kane, and five more.

Blood in a Snap — The *Finnegan's Wake* of the 21st century, by Jim Weiler and Al Gorithm

Stakeout on Millennium Drive — Award-winning Indianapolis Noir — Ian Woollen.

Dope Tales #1 — Two dope-riddled classics; *Dope Runners* by Gerald Grantham and *Death Takes the Joystick* by Phillip Condé.

Dope Tales #2 — Two more narco-classics; *The Invisible Hand* by Rex Dark and *The Smokers of Hashish* by Norman Berrow.

Dope Tales #3 — Two enchanting novels of opium by the master, Sax Rohmer. *Dope* and *The Yellow Claw.*

Tenebrae — Ernest G. Henham's 1898 horror tale brought back.

The Singular Problem of the Stygian House-Boat — Two classic tales by John Kendrick Bangs about the denizens of Hades.

Tiresias — Psychotic modern horror novel by Jonathan M. Sweet.

The One After Snelling — Kickass modern noir from Richard O'Brien.

The Sign of the Scorpion — 1935 Edmund Snell tale of oriental evil.

The House of the Vampire — 1907 poetic thriller by George S. Viereck.

An Angel in the Street — Modern hardboiled noir by Peter Genovese.

The Devil's Mistress — Scottish gothic tale by J. W. Brodie-Innes.

The Lord of Terror — 1925 mystery with master-criminal, Fantômas.

The Lady of the Terraces — 1925 adventure by E. Charles Vivian.

My Deadly Angel — 1955 Cold War drama by John Chelton

Prose Bowl — Futuristic satire — Bill Pronzini & Barry N. Malzberg .

Satan's Den Exposed — True crime in Truth or Consequences New Mexico — Award-winning journalism by the *Desert Journal*.

The Amorous Intrigues & Adventures of Aaron Burr — by Anonymous — Hot historical action.

I Stole $16,000,000 — A true story by cracksman Herbert E. Wilson.

The Black Dark Murders — Vintage 50s college murder yarn by Milt Ozaki, writing as Robert O. Saber.

Sex Slave — Potboiler of lust in the days of Cleopatra — Dion Leclerq.

You'll Die Laughing — Bruce Elliott's 1945 novel of murder at a practical joker's English countryside manor.

The Private Journal & Diary of John H. Surratt — The memoirs of the man who conspired to assassinate President Lincoln.

Dead Man Talks Too Much — Hollywood boozer by Weed Dickenson

Red Light — History of legal prostitution in Shreveport Louisiana by Eric Brock. Includes wonderful photos of the houses and the ladies.

A Snark Selection — Lewis Carroll's *The Hunting of the Snark* with two Snarkian chapters by Harry Stephen Keeler — Illustrated by Gavin L. O'Keefe.

Ripped from the Headlines! — The Jack the Ripper story as told in the newspaper articles in the *New York* and *London Times*.

Geronimo — S. M. Barrett's 1905 autobiography of a noble American.

The White Peril in the Far East — Sidney Lewis Gulick's 1905 indictment of the West and assurance that Japan would never attack the U.S.

The Compleat Calhoon — All of Fender Tucker's works: Includes *The Totah Trilogy*, *Weed, Women and Song* and *Tales from the Tower*, plus a CD of all of his songs.

RAMBLE HOUSE

Fender Tucker, Prop.

www.ramblehouse.com   fender@ramblehouse.com

228-826-1783   10329 Sheephead Drive, Vancleave MS 39565

Made in the USA